SCREAM SEA

ELF GIRL and RAVEN BOY

WITHDRAWN

Also by Marcus Sedgwick
for older readers

Blood Red, Snow White
The Book of Dead Days
The Dark Flight Down
The Dark Horse
Floodland
The Foreshadowing
The Kiss of Death
Midwinterblood
Revolver
My Swordhand is Singing
White Crow
Witch Hill

The Raven Mysteries

Flood and Fang
Ghosts and Gadgets
Lunatics and Luck
Vampires and Volts
Magic and Mayhem
Diamonds and Doom

Elf Girl and Raven Boy

Fright Forest
Monster Mountains

Visit Marcus Sedgwick's website at –
www.marcussedgwick.com

and for more on the Raven Mysteries, go to –
www.ravenmysteries.co.uk

SCREAM SEA

ELF GIRL and RAVEN BOY

MARCUS SEDGWICK

Illustrated by Pete Williamson

Orion
Children's Books

First published in Great Britain in 2013
by Orion Children's Books
a division of the Orion Publishing Group Ltd
Orion House
5 Upper St Martin's Lane
London WC2H 9EA
An Hachette UK Company

3 5 7 9 10 8 6 4

T   be

CLACKMANNANSHIRE COUNCIL	
31513400210972	
Bertrams	18/12/2015
J2 SED	£6.99
ADU	JF

A catalogue record for this book is available from the British
Library.

ISBN 978 1 4440 0525 7

Printed in Great Britain by CPI Group (UK) Ltd,
Croydon, CRO 4YY

www.orionbooks.co.uk

For Tibbs and Willow

Scream Sea

The Isl

Monster Mountains

Fright Forest

Dread Desert

Terror Town

Creepy Caves

ONE

Raven Boy's favourite time of the year is the spring, when all the little baby things are born in the forest. He's a real softie.

'This isn't funny,' said Elf Girl.

Raven Boy didn't say anything. He was too hungry and too cross to even bother replying.

They were lying on a hot beach, staring out to sea.

Some people do that sort of thing for a good time, but Elf Girl and Raven Boy were having the exact opposite of a good time.

Rat was curled up on Raven Boy's head, asleep, too hot and bothered to keep his eyes open.

'I said, this isn't funny,' Elf Girl said again. She didn't like being ignored.

'I heard you the first time,' muttered Raven Boy.

'Well?' asked Elf Girl.

'Well what?'

'Well, what do you have to say?'

'About what?'

'About what I said.'

'You didn't say anything.'

'Yes, I did!' snapped Elf Girl. Her ears were getting pink but Raven Boy was too fed up to worry about Elf Girl's ears. He'd learned by now that the pinker they got, the crosser she was, but right now pink ears were the last thing on his mind.

'Nothing sensible,' he said.

'Nothing sensible?' Elf Girl said, sounding confused.

'Yes, you didn't say anything sensible. And anyway, this is a really bad conversation. In fact, it's barely a conversation at all. It's just a bunch of words.'

Elf Girl was so cross that she stood up, and put her hands on her hips. Her ears were glowing.

Raven Boy didn't say anything.

'Are you ignoring me?' demanded Elf Girl.

Rat opened an eye, and just in case, decided to slink off the top of Raven Boy's head. He skittered over to some long sea grass and poked his nose out.

Raven Boy folded his arms and stared at the sea even harder than before.

'I won't let you ignore me,' squealed Elf Girl.

She stamped her foot and her ears almost blew off the side of her head. She looked fit to burst.

'I said, you're not going to ignore me!'

Raven Boy still said nothing. Rat shut his eyes tight.

Elf Girl threw herself at Raven Boy and began to punch and kick him all at once.

'Ow!' wailed Raven Boy. 'Stop it, you're tickling . . . I . . . Ow! Hey, that hurts!

No, don't do . . . Ow!'

He wriggled free and got to his feet.

'What has got into you?' he demanded.

'What do you think, Bird Brain?'

'I'll pretend I didn't hear that,' said Raven Boy.

'Pretend all you want,' said Elf Girl. 'You are a Bird Brain! What have we been doing? Walking along this beach for days! With nothing to eat!'

'We had that sea cabbage sandwich.'

'Two days ago!' screeched Elf Girl. 'And it wouldn't have fed a dormouse! Let alone two starving people and a greedy rat!'

Rat stuck his head up and squeaked as if he'd been insulted.

'That's not fair!' said Raven Boy. 'He's got just as much right to eat as we have.'

'You know,' said Elf Girl, with an evil glint in her eye, 'there are places where they don't keep rats as pets. There are places where they eat them!'

Rat squeaked even louder.

'Right! That does it!' roared Raven Boy, and he jumped on Elf Girl and they rolled around on the sand, pinching and biting and generally behaving very, very badly.

'Stupid Bird Beak!' cried Elf Girl.

'Pointy-eared freak!' snarled Raven Boy.

They fought for a long time, and only stopped fighting when they got tired.

They both lay on their backs, staring into the sky, listening to the sound of the waves on the shore.

'I'm sorry,' said Elf Girl, finally.

Raven Boy turned onto his side and looked at her.

'So am I,' he said. 'This is all so hard.'

'Saving the world?'

'Yes,' he said, nodding. 'We still have so much to do and such a long way to go. We don't know what the Singing Sword is, or the Tears of the Moon. We don't know where they are either. All we do know is that we have to cross that sea to find the Goblin King, and that we need the Sword and the Tears to defeat him.'

'And,' added Elf Girl, 'we've got no food, and no money to buy any. All we have is a stupid bow and three little magic wands that can only be used once each.'

They'd found six of these magic wands in the wizard's castle, high in the Monster Mountains. They'd already used the first three to zap Bob and Bert and Cedric, the three hungry trolls who'd followed them all the way from Fright Forest. They might still be on their trail, even though Elf Girl had set their bottoms alight with the wands. Trolls, as everyone knows, are mean and warty and ugly and these three were intent on putting Elf Girl and Raven Boy in their cooking pot.

'Oh, Raven Boy, it's impossible. We'll never do it!'

Raven Boy didn't have the heart to disagree with her.

'You didn't mean that, did you?' he said instead. 'About Rat?'

'No,' said Elf Girl. Her cheeks went pink as she remembered what she'd said. 'I'm sorry, I shouldn't have said it.'

'You should say sorry to him,' said Raven Boy, gently.

'Yes, I suppose I should . . . Only, where

is he?'

Raven Boy looked around.

He stood up.

'Rat?' he called. 'Rat! Where are you?'

Elf Girl stood up too and they hunted around in the sea grass, calling out to Rat to stop hiding, but he was nowhere to be seen.

'Oh,' said Elf Girl, 'look!'

She pointed at the sand, where a trail of rat-like footprints led away along the beach.

'You don't think he . . . '

'I think he might have been very upset by what you said,' said Raven Boy. 'Come on! We have to find him and then you have to make him feel like the best rat in the whole world.'

'Yes!' said Elf Girl. 'I really didn't mean it! I was just cross with you . . . But I promise! Come on, let's hurry. He can't have gone far.'

So they set off, as fast as they could manage, along the beach, in pursuit of their small furry friend.

Two

Elf Girl once spent two days trying to decide whether her dress matched her shoes.

'There he is!' cried Raven Boy.

They had run over a sand dune and were looking across another wide, empty patch of sand.

'Where? Behind that clump of seaweed?'

'Oh,' said Raven Boy sadly, 'I thought the seaweed was him.'

'There, look! Is that him?'

Raven Boy peered into the distance, and there, heading over the brow of a golden dune, was the little shape of Rat.

'Wait!' cried Raven Boy.

They scampered down the dune and headed after him. Elf Girl was feeling very bad indeed.

'Can't you stop him with your bow?' cried Raven Boy as they ran.

'No! I might fry him by mistake. You know I don't really know what I'm doing with it yet.'

'That's true enough,' muttered Raven Boy, remembering being turned into a block of ice by one of Elf Girl's mistakes.

'What did you say?' asked Elf Girl.

'Nothing! Nothing!' Raven Boy smiled. 'Come on, we must be catching him up now.'

'He moves fast for a little thing,' panted Elf Girl as she ran.

It was tricky running on the sand and trickier still to clamber to the top of the big sand dune Rat had skipped up and over. The heat made it even worse, so they were both exhausted when finally they made it to the top.

When they did, they stopped dead.

'Oh!' cried Elf Girl. 'Look! We're saved!'

'All that walking and nothing . . . And now this!'

Ahead of them lay a busy town, a port in fact, with a harbour full of colourful boats. Around the harbour the town spread out towards them, with streets full of houses and shops and inns.

'Clever Rat!' cried Raven Boy. 'Only, where is he?'

There was a squeak and they both spun round to see Rat behind them.

He squeaked a bit, and Elf Girl looked sheepish.

'Is he saying what I think he's saying?' she asked Raven Boy.

Raven Boy nodded.

'Yes, but he's not that impressed with me, either. He thinks we're both a bit useless, to be honest.'

Elf Girl nodded solemnly.

'Rat,' she said. 'You're right; we are useless. And I didn't mean what I said about eating you. It was because I was cross with Raven Boy and how useless he is . . . '

Rat began squeaking again, as loudly as they'd ever heard him.

'Yes, yes,' said Elf Girl. 'We're both useless. And anyway, I'm really sorry, and anyway again, that doesn't matter now, because you've saved us and found this town. So now we can get something to eat and a bed to sleep in and find a ship to cross the sea.'

Raven Boy waited for Elf Girl to finish.

'What?' she said, as she saw him looking at her.

'That's all great,' he said, 'only we still don't have any money.'

'Raven Boy!' cried Elf Girl. 'Don't be so glum! We'll just have to get some money, won't we?'

'Get some?' asked Raven Boy. He looked puzzled. 'How do you get money?'

'Well, you work for it,' said Elf Girl. 'I think.'

She looked puzzled too.

'Work? And then people give you money?' asked Raven Boy.

Elf Girl nodded.

'Crazy world,' said Raven Boy. 'Why not just eat what the forest has on offer? And sleep in a tree?'

'Because we're not in a forest, in case you hadn't noticed! And because not everyone is happy with nut pie every single meal. That's why! Some people want to eat more interesting things . . . '

Rat squeaked again, and his tail quivered.

' . . . like lots of other really yummy things made from vegetables,' said Elf Girl, quickly.

She smiled at Rat, who glared back at her.

'Anyway,' she went on, 'whether you understand it or not, that's how most people get money. They work for it. So we'll find someone to work for, get some money, and then we can eat, and sleep in a bed.'

'Okay,' said Raven Boy. 'Though I'm still not sure about sleeping in a bed. I would like something to eat, though . . . '

'Good. At least we agree on that. And then we can find a ship that's crossing the sea, yes?'

'Yes,' said Raven Boy. 'Look! There's a nice big one now, coming into port. That looks like the sort of ship we want.'

'A nice big one?' laughed Elf Girl. 'You know a lot about ships, do you?'

Raven Boy scowled at her.

'Let's go down and see what's what.'

They set off towards the seaside town. Rat decided it was time to stop sulking, and climbed back up onto Raven Boy's head, though he made sure he dug his claws in a bit so Raven Boy would know he was there.

Very soon they'd reached the first houses. Raven Boy wandered along as if he'd never seen a town, which he hadn't. Even Elf Girl felt like a bumpkin from the country, because she'd never seen anything so grand before.

The houses were bigger than anything she'd seen, but strangely they couldn't see anyone on the streets, though it was the middle of the day.

'Well,' said Raven Boy, 'how do we start?'

'Easy,' said Elf Girl. 'We just ask someone for a job, and they give us one. Watch.'

She went up to the nearest door, and knocked on it.

There was no answer, so she tried another door.

There was no answer at that one either, so she tried a third.

This time, the door opened, and a grumpy-looking woman peered out.

'What?' she said.

'Err, please may we have a job?' said Elf Girl, as brightly as she could.

The woman made a short, loud sound, a bit like a dog barking.

'Hah!' she said. 'A job! Are you trying to be funny?'

She shut the door in their faces.

Elf Girl looked at Raven Boy.

'I think,' she said, 'this might not be as easy as I thought.'

THREE

Rat's favourite food is anything he hasn't had to find for himself. He's a bit lazy that way.

Elf Girl was right.

It wasn't easy. Not easy at all. They knocked on lots of doors, and while some people just shut the door, others shouted and told them to clear off.

They were beginning to feel very miserable,
when finally an old man took pity on them.

'It's not their fault,' he explained. He was
talking about the townspeople. He stood on his
doorstep and told Elf Girl and Raven Boy why
everyone was so grumpy.

'There's no work for anyone,' he said.
'This is a fishing town. And there are no fish
in the sea. For weeks the fishermen have been
coming back with empty nets. They've been
going farther and farther out too, almost as far
as Scream Sea, and still they've found nothing.'

Scream Sea? thought Raven Boy. That sounds scary.

'Why aren't there any fish?' asked Elf Girl.

The old man scratched his head.

'It's the work of the Goblin King! He's stealing all the fish from the sea.'

At the sound of the evil Goblin King's name, Elf Girl and Raven Boy opened their eyes wide.

'So you've heard of him?' asked the old man.

'He sent an ogre to pull down the forest where we live!' cried Raven Boy.

'I see,' said the old man. 'That's what they say. That he's the one responsible for all the fish disappearing. We all rely on fish – everyone. So no fish, no work. You'd do better to give up and move along.'

'But we can't!' wailed Elf Girl. 'We have nowhere to go. And we have to cross Scream Sea to go and find the Goblin King and stop him doing all these bad things.'

The old man looked thoughtful for a minute.

'Well,' he said. 'Well. You're going to try and stop the Goblin King? Across Scream Sea? Maybe I can help you after all.'

'Would you? That would be very kind of you.'

The old man nodded.

'We can't have you starving to death now, can we? Come along to the tavern, and I'll buy you something to eat and drink.'

Elf Girl and Raven Boy thanked the man again and again as they walked through the deserted town to an old tavern by the docks.

It stood next to the harbour wall, and was called The Mermaid's Tail.

The kind old man bustled inside, and Raven Boy and Elf Girl followed. Rat hid inside Raven Boy's pocket, in case there were people who didn't like rats, which was something, he had found, that was very common.

He needn't have worried, because the tavern was empty. Not a soul. It was a dark and dusty place, and despite the hot day outside, was cold and gloomy inside.

Eventually, the landlord appeared and

nodded at the old man.

'Ah, there you are,' he said. 'Now Jack, I want to buy these two young people a nice hot meal and a drink of something lovely. Can you do that?'

Jack, the landlord, raised an eyebrow.

'Very well, but we don't have fish.'

'I know you don't have fish,' snapped the old man. 'No one has fish. That's obvious. But you must have something else.'

'I could make vegetable soup,' said Jack.

'I'd be happier with soup anyway,' said Raven Boy.

'Shh,' hushed Elf Girl. 'Be grateful.'

'I am grateful,' said Raven Boy. 'But you know I don't like to eat anything with a face.'

'Do fish have faces?' asked Elf Girl.

'I don't know,' said Raven Boy. 'I guess they do.'

The old man waved Elf Girl and Raven Boy to a table.

'Now you two just sit here and Jack will be back with some food.'

'Thank you, sir,' said Raven Boy. 'It's

really very kind of you.'

The old man seemed to be thinking about something.

'You know, if you really want to cross the sea, I might be able to help you with that too.'

'Really?' asked Elf Girl.

'Really,' said the man. 'Wait here while I go and have a quick chat with a friend of mine. Ship's captain. He just came in to port. I'll see what I can do.'

'Oh, thank you,' said Raven Boy, 'thank you so much.'

Jack came back with some really good lemonade for them, and the old man shuffled out of The Mermaid's Tail, saying, 'Now don't you be going anywhere. I'll be five minutes.'

The vegetable soup was excellent and the lemonade was even better. Once Jack the landlord had left them alone, Rat poked his nose out and had a little drink of lemonade and a lick of the soup.

Soon, all three of them were feeling much better about life.

'This is all very nice, isn't it?' said Raven Boy.

'Such a friendly old man,' agreed Elf Girl. 'Only we still have to cross Scream Sea, and I have to say that sounds a bit scary.'

'I agree,' said Raven Boy. He sighed. 'Why do we never find anywhere called Fluffy Field? Or Lovely Lane?'

Elf Girl giggled.

'Or Marvellous Meadows?'

Raven Boy laughed.

'I've got one!' he said, sniggering. 'Brilliant Beach.'

Elf Girl snorted.

'Peaceful Pond,' she squeaked between guffaws, and then they both sat giggling like loons for a while. Suddenly, Elf Girl stopped laughing and sat bolt upright.

'You know what, though, Raven Boy?'

'What?'

'There's something about this that worries me.'

'What do you mean?'

'I was just thinking,' explained Elf Girl, 'about the last time we were really hungry, in the forest, and then those three men offered us food, and then they turned out to be trolls and you know how that ended . . . '

'Eep,' muttered Raven Boy.

'Yes, eep . . . ' said Elf Girl, but she didn't get any further, for at that very moment, the old man banged back into the tavern, and with him was a tall and strong man. He was obviously a sailor and they guessed he was the captain of the ship.

He had big shoulders, and wore a fancy jacket with shiny metal bits.

The old man nodded at them, and turned to the captain.

'There they are. What do you think?'

The captain walked over to Raven Boy and Elf Girl, and looked them up and down.

'Are you a ship's captain?' asked Raven Boy.

The captain ignored him. Instead, he whistled and two more big sailors came into the tavern. They looked very strong too. The captain

went back over to the old man.

'Fifty,' he said.

'What?' roared the old man. 'Two hundred!'

'Raven Boy,' whispered Elf Girl. 'What's
going on?'

Raven Boy opened his mouth; nothing
came out.

'Two hundred?' sneered the captain. 'Sixty.'

'Sixty? Are you trying to rob me?' asked the old man. 'A hundred and fifty.'

'Don't make me laugh. And anyway, I'm not robbing you since they're not yours anyway. I don't have to pay you anything, so I suggest you take my final offer. Which is forty.'

'What?' shouted the old man. 'You offered me sixty a second ago!'

'So I did, but then I realised that I don't like you, so it went down. And I can make my offer even lower if you . . . '

'Fine! Fine, I'll take forty.'

The old man held his hand out, and the captain fished in his pocket for a bag of coins. He counted four of them into the old man's hand.

'Sold,' he said.

Raven Boy and Elf Girl looked at each other.

'Sold?' wailed Elf Girl.

'Sold!' laughed the old man, and wandered out of the tavern counting his four coins again and again.

'Right,' said the captain. 'Get 'em on board!'

Four

Rat is extremely good at hiding super-quick if he has to. It's a sad fact that many people Do Not Like Rats.

Elf Girl looked at Raven Boy and Raven Boy looked at Elf Girl. They did that for about a second, and then they both screamed as the sailors headed towards them.

'Elf Girl!' shrieked Raven Boy. 'Use your bow!'

'Right!' cried Elf Girl, and quick as a flash, she grabbed her bow from where she'd propped it against the table, and stretched its invisible string.

She aimed at the closest of the two, shut her eyes, and the invisible string suddenly appeared, glowing red.

All this happened so quickly, the sailors didn't even have time to wonder what she was doing. There was a blinding flash and suddenly the two sailors had vanished, and two little pink piglets were oinking about on the floor of The Mermaid's Tail.

'Holy monkey brains!' shouted the captain, and ducked out of the door.

'You did it!' cried Raven Boy. 'Yay! You did it!'

'Err . . . ' said Elf Girl, because before she could say anything else, the captain reappeared, shoving another seven of his crew in front of him.

'I just spent your pay on these two,' he snarled, 'so you'd better catch them! Sharpish!'

The sailors charged towards Elf Girl and Raven Boy, and Rat scurried away to hide, just as Elf Girl let fly once more with her magic bow.

With her first try she managed to cover two of them in porridge, which confused them so much they fell over.

'I think pigs was a better idea,' said Raven Boy.

'Shut up, Raven Boy!' yelled Elf Girl. 'I don't know what I'm doing! Help me! Use the magic wands!'

With that, she aimed again and turned two of the other three sailors into pigs, while Raven Boy pulled out the three wands and took aim.

'You see!' he called to Elf Girl. 'You do know what you're doing!'

With the first two wands he zapped two sailors, setting their trousers on fire, but then missed with the third.

'I promise you I don't,' shouted Elf Girl, as the last sailor came forwards.

He was hesitating, having seen what Elf Girl had done, but the captain gave him a kick in the seat of his pants.

'Get a move on!' he roared, 'or I'll feed you to the sharks!'

With that, the sailor rushed at Elf Girl, who fired once more, and where there had been a sailor, there was suddenly a giant puff of smoke, out of which emerged a small, bright green parrot. The parrot looked confused and flapped off into the tavern somewhere.

'EEP!' cried Raven Boy. 'Look out!'

He pointed to where the first two sailors had wiped the porridge from their eyes and were making ready to charge again, though one of them fell over a piglet, just as Elf Girl fired, managing to turn them both into little pink pigs. Little pink piglets covered in porridge, in fact, which they began to lick off each other happily.

'Yes!' cheered Raven Boy. He jumped for joy and was about to hug Elf Girl, when something bopped him on the head. As he saw stars fizzing, he noticed Jack the landlord bopping Elf Girl on the head from behind with a large bottle of lemonade.

'Oh, nuts,' sighed Raven Boy as everything went black and he fell to the floor.

Elf Girl slid down on top of him.

'Nice work, Jack,' said the captain. 'Now, I'll just be getting what's left of my crew out of here.'

He flipped a dirty coin at Jack, who bit it to see if it was real and then said a bad word because he'd chipped a tooth.

'All right,' he said. 'Just make sure you get all that porridge off my floor first.'

He needn't have worried about that, because six little piglets were making short work of it, all watched by a confused parrot.

FIVE

For as long as he can remember, Raven Boy has had dreams that he can fly, and thinks he might have been a bird in a former life.

Raven Boy opened his eyes.

Something was wrong.

For a start, the floor was moving. He knew that because he was lying on it.

He looked about and took it in all at once. It was like being in a cramped bedroom, with a table, a chair, wooden floor and walls, and one round window. And there was Elf Girl, lying a little way away from him on the floor.

He crawled over to her and shook her shoulders.

'Elf Girl! Elf Girl? Are you alive? Say something!'

She opened her eyes.

'Stop shaking me,' she said. Then, 'Why is the floor moving?'

'I don't know,' said Raven Boy, 'but I'm so pleased you're all right.'

'All right?' snapped Elf Girl. 'I have a terrible headache, and . . . ow . . . a bump on the back of my head.'

'So do I,' said Raven Boy. 'That landlord bopped us on the head, right after—'

'Eep!' cried Elf Girl. 'Yes, I remember now! Right after that nice old man turned out to be a mean and nasty and horrible old man, and sold us!'

'That still doesn't explain why the floor is moving,' said Raven Boy.

'Doesn't it?' asked Elf Girl, getting up and going to the window.

'Look!' she declared. 'We're at sea!'

Elf Girl had a habit of getting things

exactly right from time to time, and this was one of those times.

Raven Boy stared out of the window for three seconds, without saying a word, and then fainted on the floor again.

When he woke up, Elf Girl was sitting on the bed, swinging her feet as if she was bored.

'Raven Boy, wake up!' she said, as she saw him blinking on the floor. 'We have to work out what to do.'

'B-but . . . ' stuttered Raven Boy, 'we're at sea.'

'We are far out to sea, Raven Boy. Miles and miles. There's no sign of land at all.'

'MEEP,' meeped Raven Boy. 'Where's Rat?'

'I have no idea,' said Elf Girl. 'And my bow's missing too. We're on some ship or other, and the door's locked, by the way. All in all, this is looking like the worst situation we've faced.'

'What? Even worse than being eaten by trolls?'

'Yes. And, anyway, we didn't actually get eaten, did we?'

'That's true,' said Raven Boy. 'But we

nearly did.'

'Come on, Raven Boy!' cried Elf Girl. 'Do something!'

'What? What can I do? It's not as if there are any animals around that I can ask for help.'

'Maybe you could hang out of the window and try and talk to a passing haddock?'

Raven Boy was about to give a very rude answer to that suggestion, when there was a rattling of a key in the lock, and the door opened.

In walked the captain, accompanied by three tough-looking sailors. Now that they saw the captain again, Raven Boy decided he liked the look of him even less. He had three golden teeth, and his hair, which was long and curly, looked as though it hadn't been washed in a fair while. He was holding Elf Girl's bow.

The three sailors were even grubbier and even smellier. One had a shaven head, a few teeth missing and was very short. He looked as if he might be very stupid. The other two were taller, and had mean looks on their faces, as though they couldn't wait to do something unpleasant.

'So!' said the captain. 'You're awake! It's about time.'

That made Raven Boy cross.

'Well, you shouldn't go bopping people on the head if you don't want them to be unconscious all afternoon.'

'You're not people,' said the captain. 'You're goods. I bought you, and until I sell you again, I can do whatever I want with you, see?'

'No,' said Elf Girl, 'we do not see. And give me back my bow.'

'Give you back your bow? After you turned half my crew into living sausages? Not likely.'

The captain handed the bow to the short sailor.

'Hold that, Billy,' he said, 'while I tell them a thing or two.'

The captain stalked over, towering above their heads.

'Now listen here!' he roared. 'My name is Captain Scrim, and this is my ship, the *Naughty Porpoise*! I'm in charge here and everyone aboard does exactly what I tell them. And that includes you! So right now, you're going to tell me how to work this magic bow of yours, and if you do, I might just let you live! Get it?'

Captain Scrim was a bit red in the face by the time he'd finished yelling at them, and stood back, first to see if he'd scared them properly, and secondly so he could get his breath back.

As it happened, Raven Boy was feeling very scared indeed, but when he turned to Elf Girl, he noticed that her ears were deep pink.

'No!' she said, 'I do not get it! You have not bought us! What are you thinking? That bow is mine and you are going to give it back, and if you don't, we're going to report you for being very naughty sailors. Isn't that right, Raven Boy?'

Elf Girl turned to Raven Boy, who smiled a faint smile at the captain.

'Please don't upset her,' he said, timidly.

Captain Scrim turned to his crew.

'Oh, these two take the cake, they really do. Haven't had such fun with a pair of slaves in quite a while.'

'Slaves?' cried Elf Girl. 'Who are you calling slaves?'

'You!' bellowed the captain. 'And let me correct you about a few other things. Yes, you're slaves, and I own you, at least I do until I sell you again. We know a nice little island where we'll get a good price for you. Which is just as well, given the trouble you've caused me!'

He pointed a grimy finger at Elf Girl's nose.

'And one more thing,' he whispered. 'We ain't sailors. Oh no. We're pirates, see? Pirates! So do the sensible thing, and scream!'

And with that, the captain whipped out a sharp-looking sword and waved it at Elf Girl, who did the sensible thing, and screamed herself silly.

Six

There are many uses for one-use wands, but it's a bit of a waste to make cheese on toast with them.

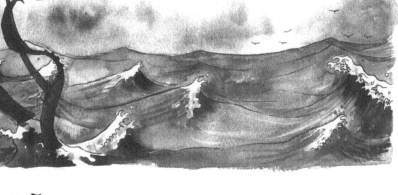

While Elf Girl screamed, Raven Boy did his best to look worried which, to be honest, was pretty easy.

Captain Scrim, meanwhile, leaned back against the table and chuckled, while the other pirates grinned and made faces at each other. They were all sure that there would be some nasty stuff to get up to very soon.

'Pirates?' was what Elf Girl gasped when

she'd stopped screaming.

'You catch on fast,' said the captain, and they all laughed in a mean way.

'And what are you going to do with us?'

'I told you,' sighed Captain Scrim. 'You're going to tell us how to use the magic bow. And then we're going to sell you for a nice fat profit on a little island I know. We're heading there right now.'

'But I can't,' said Elf Girl. 'I can't tell you how to use my bow. Even if I wanted to. Which I don't. But even if I did, I couldn't.'

'What's she on about?' snapped the captain, looking suddenly very fiercely at Raven Boy.

'She can't tell you. She doesn't know how to use it.'

'But she turned my crew into pigs!'

'I get lucky sometimes!' cried Elf Girl. 'I couldn't do it again if you paid me. And for all I know, the bow wouldn't work for pirates anyway.'

'Do you expect me to believe all this bilge?' asked the captain. He looked as if he might be about to get angry again.

'It's true!' cried Raven Boy. 'It's no good shouting at us; she still won't know how to use it!'

'Nonsense!' declared the captain. 'She turned Alfred into a parrot. She knows exactly

what she's doing, and she's going to tell me!'

'Never!' cried Elf Girl.

'We'll see,' said Captain Scrim. 'Boys! Take them and throw them in the hold. Let's see what a day or two below decks does to them.'

The captain stomped off, and the sailors grabbed Elf Girl and Raven Boy, and marched out of the cabin.

On deck, Raven Boy got his first proper view of the sea, and it nearly made him faint again. There was nothing at all, nothing as far as the eye could see, in any direction. Just wave after wave of wobbly blue water. It made him pine for the trees of his forest home. For the little creatures he'd chat to, the ravens and woodpeckers, the squirrels and the badgers, and it made him long for strawberry pie and elderberry water.

But there was no time to think about these things, because they were being taken under the wooden deck of the ship. Dodging a couple of stray pigs, the three sailors shoved Elf Girl down a steep flight of steps that led below deck. Once she'd gone, it was Raven Boy's turn. The steps were so steep it was more like climbing a ladder, but Raven Boy is very good at climbing and soon he was in a dark space. Fortunately, his excellent night vision meant he could see everything. Unfortunately, Elf Girl couldn't.

'Ow!' she said, bumping her head. On Raven Boy.

'Ow!' he said, and then there was a scraping noise and the steps were pulled up, leaving them in the dark and smelly bottom of the ship.

'MEEP!' said Raven Boy quietly.

'Come on, Raven Boy,' said Elf Girl. 'That's not going to help us much, is it?'

'Well, what do you have to say for yourself?' asked Raven Boy. 'Do you have any ideas?'

Elf Girl said nothing for a long time, while she thought about Raven Boy's words, and then she said something so quietly, Raven Boy had to ask her to say it again.

'MEEP,' she said. 'All right, I admit it. We're stuck and stumped, for sure, this time.'

They sat down on the floor in the dark, and waited for something to happen.

When nothing did, Raven Boy stood up again.

'I'm going to try and find out where we are,' he said.

Even with his excellent night vision, now that the trapdoor was shut, there was no light at all, none, and without a little bit of moonlight like there'd be in the forest, he was as blind as blind.

He began to walk with his hands out in front of him, waiting to bump into something. It didn't take very long for him to find a wall, and then he turned and followed the wall, turning at each corner.

Each corner, as it turned out, was very soon after the last one, and Raven Boy decided they were in a very small space, very small indeed.

'I'd be surprised if we can both lie down in here,' he said.

'And why would I want to lie down in here?' asked Elf Girl.

'Because you might want to sleep,' said

Raven Boy.

'And why would I want to do that?' she persisted.

'Because we might be in here for a very long time,' Raven Boy explained.

'Might we?' asked Elf Girl.

'I think we might,' said Raven Boy, sadly. 'I think we might be locked down here, with no hope, and no idea where we're going, or how to get out.'

'Raven Boy,' said Elf Girl, 'I'm scared. And fed up, all at once. What can we do?'

Raven Boy was about to admit that he didn't have a clue, when, in the dark, they heard a sound they knew well, and loved even more.

A squeak.

'Rat!' cried Raven Boy. 'Is that you? It is! Oh Rat, are we pleased to see you.'

Rat squeaked again.

'No, I know we can't see you,' said Raven Boy, 'but it's wonderful just to hear you! Hooray for Rat!'

'Yay!' cried Elf Girl.

And Rat squeaked once more, though in

his little rat head, he wasn't really any clearer about how to get them out of the ship's hold than they were.

Seven

**True troll fact: Trolls smell worse
on Wednesdays.**

'They can't keep us down here for ever,' said
Raven Boy.

They stared into the darkness.

Three days later, Elf Girl said, 'Are you
sure about that?'

Every now and again, one of the pirates
lifted the lid of the hatch and threw a bit of
bread down to them, bread so old it was furry.
Or a flask of warm water. Then the hatch

would slide shut again and they'd hear a bolt being drawn across.

As the fourth day dawned, Raven Boy and Elf Girl were getting desperate.

It was only because Rat was there that they didn't go mad, or start fighting each other, or both.

He'd sneak up out of the hold and run around the ship, taking great care not to be seen by anyone. Once a day, at least, he'd run around listening to what the pirates were saying and then he'd report back to Raven Boy.

After one trip, Rat was full of news, and squeaked as though someone had trod on his tail.

Raven Boy explained what he'd said.

'He says it's only another day to Blackheart Isle. That's where they're taking us.'

'To sell? asked Elf Girl.

'I'm afraid so,' said Raven Boy. 'And Blackheart Isle doesn't sound the nicest place ever. But that's not the worst of it.'

'Not the worst!' exclaimed Elf Girl.

Rat was squeaking still, with his fur all fluffed up, he was so excited. Raven Boy could barely keep up.

'He says . . . He says . . . Oh! He says that Blackheart Isle is in the control of the Goblin King! If we get sold there, we'll be in his power! Then there'll be nothing we can do to stop him! Nothing!'

Elf Girl made a gurgling noise in her throat.

'Ulp,' she said, eventually. 'We're doomed!'

'Don't give up,' said Raven Boy. 'We still have another day to escape.'

'But how?' cried Elf Girl. 'We're stuck down here.'

'Maybe Rat could chew through the walls for us . . . '

Rat squeaked. It wasn't a happy squeak.

'Well?' asked Elf Girl.

'He says it would take him a month. The planks of the ship are so thick.'

'We have to do something. We only have a day left.'

'Maybe we can try pleading,' said Raven Boy. 'Or begging. Or you could try crying and I could try sobbing.'

'Raven Boy,' said Elf Girl, 'that's the

dumbest idea I've ever heard, and anyway, I refuse to cry in front of those nasty pirates. I simply refuse.'

'Wow,' said Raven Boy. 'You're very brave.'

Elf Girl didn't feel brave. She sat in the dark and was glad Raven Boy couldn't see her properly, so he couldn't see that she was shaking.

'If only I had my bow,' she said after a while.

'Yes, but Captain Nasty has it. And you're making him super mad by not telling him how to use it.'

'But I can't, can I? And even if I could, I wouldn't.'

'Can't you give him some idea? Then maybe he'd let us go.'

'I don't think so, Raven Boy. I think he's going to sell us no matter what.'

'But I didn't like what he said yesterday.'

'Yesterday?'

'Yes, yesterday. You know. When he said that if you didn't tell him by the time we got to the island, he'd pull my toes off until you told him.'

'I don't think he meant that,' said Elf Girl.

'I'd rather not find out, if it's all the same to you. Couldn't you tell him something at least? Make it up, just to buy us time? He'll be back before too long.'

That was true.

Captain Scrim had been visiting them once a day, squinting down through the hatch, and demanding to be told how the bow worked.

He'd obviously been trying to use it, but hadn't got it to do a thing. Not one thing. Not even make another piglet.

Just then, there was the sound of the bolt being drawn back, and the hatch slid open.

Bright sunlight poured into the hold, and Elf Girl and Raven Boy sat blinking, shielding their eyes from the light.

'So!' roared Scrim. 'This is your last chance. Tell me how the bow works, or it's no more toes for the bird boy!'

Maybe he does mean it, thought Elf Girl, desperately trying to come up with a plan.

'All right,' she said, 'but you have to promise not to hurt us if I do.'

'I promise no such thing. But I promise I'll pull all *your* toes off as well if you don't tell me! Right now!'

'Okay, okay,' said Elf Girl, thinking fast. 'It's like this. In order to make the bow work, you have to think really nice thoughts. Nice ones. If you're not thinking totally and completely lovely things in your head when you use it, nothing happens. Nothing at all.'

The captain listened to all of this with his mouth hanging open, all his gold teeth glinting in the sunlight.

'Nice thoughts?' he roared. He roared a lot.

'Nice. It's a nice bow, made by nice elves.'

'But . . . But, I don't know any nice thoughts! I'm an evil pirate captain! I don't know how to think nice!'

'You'll have to,' said Elf Girl, almost believing it herself. 'If you want to make it work, you're going to have to learn how to think nice things.'

'Garrr!' said Scrim.

'I feel sorry for you,' Elf Girl went on. 'So I'll help you. Try thinking about fluffy bunnies. Lots of them. It's very hard to be mean if you're thinking about fluffy bunnies.'

With that, the lid slid shut again, with a bang, and they were plunged into darkness once more.

'Elf Girl!' whispered Raven Boy, 'you're a genius! He'll never do it!'

'Exactly, but he'll keep trying. It should buy us some time, at least.'

'But time's what we don't have. By tomorrow, we'll be sold as slaves on Blackheart Isle.'

All three of them fell silent again, pondering their gloomy fate.

EIGHT

It's not as easy to be a pirate as some people think. You have to take all sorts of exams to prove you're scary enough. And that you don't get sea sick.

The day wore on.

Rat went exploring again, searching for some way of getting his friends out of the trouble they were in.

Around teatime, one of the crew chucked a slice of dried bread down to them, and they glumly chewed it in silence.

Then, suddenly, they heard shouts. They couldn't hear what was being said – the voices were muffled – but there was a lot of running about and all they could hear for a long time was the sound of boots thundering on the wooden deck.

It was so loud, it was like living inside a drum, and they covered their ears.

Rat scuttled down, and explained what was going on.

'He says they've found another prisoner,' Raven Boy told Elf Girl. 'They saw someone in the sea and hauled her out.'

'Who?' asked Elf Girl.

'Rat doesn't know. They're all happy, though.'

'Why?'

'Another slave to sell, of course. The captain says it will make them all very, very rich.'

'Why?' asked Elf Girl. 'What's so special about her? Why's she worth so much?'

'I don't know,' said Raven Boy. 'Rat says she's a bit smelly and skinny and her dress is all tattered. He can't understand what all the fuss is about.'

But there was a fuss. A great fuss.

Even from beneath the deck, Raven Boy and Elf Girl could hear shouts of joy and laughter that went on for the rest of the afternoon. As night fell, it still hadn't finished, and if anything got worse.

Then they heard music. Someone was playing a fiddle and someone else an accordion. The sound of stomping boots got even louder.

The pirates were dancing!

Rat scampered up to have a look around.

When he came back, he told them the pirates were having a big party. They were dancing and singing, and drinking rum. Lots of it.

The noise got louder and louder, and went on and on, into the night, and then it got louder still, as the hatch slid open once more and Captain Scrim shouted down to them.

'Fluffy bunnies?' he asked.

His voice sounded a bit funny.

'He's drunk,' whispered Elf Girl.

'Like when you have too much strawberry wine?' asked Raven Boy.

'Yes, but I think it's probably worse on rum.'

'I said, fluffy bunnies?' the captain asked again. 'Are you sure about that?'

'Oh yes,' said Elf Girl, nodding furiously.

'Hmmm,' said the captain. 'I'll have to try a bit harder then. To be nice.'

And off he went.

'Look!' cried Raven Boy. 'Look! He's left the hatch open! This is our chance.'

'Yes,' said Elf Girl, 'but we can't get out now! They're all just up there, on deck.'

It was true. Raven Boy nodded, and they sat down to wait, hoping that all the pirates had drunk too much rum to notice that the hatch was open.

The party went on, and on, and on, and Raven Boy wondered how anyone could be so loud for so long.

Eventually it started to get a bit quieter, then quieter still, and finally, all they could hear from up on deck was the sound of snoring. Lots of it.

'Now what?' asked Elf Girl.

'Now, you stand on my shoulders, and reach for the edge of the hatch.'

'I'm not tall enough!'

'You'll have to be. There's no other way.'

Elf Girl started to clamber up on to Raven Boy's back.

'Ow!' he said.

'Sorry, I'm not as good at climbing as you,' Elf Girl said.

'But you're lighter than me, so it has to be you on top. Just try and be more careful.'

Elf Girl did, and with a few wobbles, she

suddenly found herself standing on Raven Boy's shoulders.

'Quick!' she said. 'Quick! I can't keep up here for long. Left a bit and I think I can grab it!'

Raven Boy staggered to his left, and Elf Girl reached for the hatch.

'Got it!' she cried, just as she slipped from Raven Boy's shoulders.

She dangled there for a moment.

'Pull yourself up!' cried Raven Boy. 'Quick! Before you fall down!'

With great effort, Elf Girl managed to haul herself up onto the deck. It was a bright starlit night, and she could see almost as easily as by day. She looked around and saw nothing but sleeping pirates, everywhere. To her left, her right, even above her in the crow's nest, nothing but snoring sailors.

'MEEP!' came Raven Boy's voice from below.

'Yes, yes,' whispered Elf Girl and, finding a rope, she tied it to the mast, and lowered the end down for Raven Boy, who shimmied up it in no time at all, with Rat on his head.

'My, you're a good climber,' said Elf Girl. 'I'm impressed. Not bad for a boy.'

Raven Boy bowed solemnly.

'That's what happens when you live in trees.'

'Now what?' asked Elf Girl.

'Now, we get off. They must have a jolly boat for going ashore in. Let's find it, and set ourselves free!'

'Wait! We have to find my bow first.'

'Elf Girl! We don't have time. They could wake up at any moment!'

'I'm not going without it,' Elf Girl said, and her ears started to glow in the darkness.

Raven Boy sighed. He knew there was no point in arguing.

'We'll have to hurry,' he said.

They were about to start looking when, suddenly, they heard a voice.

NINE

Elf Girl's favourite place in the forest was her hut. Until Raven Boy squashed it. She'd give anything to see it put back just the way it was.

From just a way down the deck, someone was calling to them.

They could tell straight away that it wasn't a pirate, or even a pig, or a parrot.

For one thing, it was the voice of a young girl, and for another thing, what it had said was, 'Help!'

Raven Boy and Elf Girl were halfway towards the captain's cabin when they saw who it was: the new prisoner the pirates had been so delighted to capture.

'We have to help her!' said Raven Boy.

'Do we?' said Elf Girl.

Rat squeaked. He always felt sorry for the little person.

'Elf Girl, you know we have to help her,' said Raven Boy. 'That's our job, isn't it?'

'Yes, I know,' said Elf Girl. 'Sorry.'

They tiptoed over to the girl. She was tiny, and thin, even tinier and thinner than Elf Girl, and she was wearing a very tatty dress. If they hadn't known better, they would have sworn it was made from seaweed.

'Oh, please help me!'

said the girl. 'They're going to sell me!'

'They were going to sell us, too,' said
Raven Boy, smiling at her. 'But actually we're
going to escape! Of course we'll help you, won't
we, Elf Girl?'

Elf Girl folded her arms.

'Have you forgotten about my bow?' she
hissed at Raven Boy.

'Please get me out of these chains,' said
the girl. 'Please? I want to go home.'

'Yes,' said Raven Boy, 'but how? They're
locked with a padlock and we can't cut through
chains.'

'The captain has the key!' whispered the
girl. 'Please! Hurry!'

'And he has your bow too,' said Raven
Boy, and Elf Girl unfolded her arms.

They crept towards the captain's cabin,
pulling the door open as quietly as they could.

Rat stayed with the girl, and decided she
might feel better if he sat on her head, so he did.
Her tangled hair was rather salty, he decided,
but otherwise quite comfortable.

Elf Girl and Raven Boy found the captain,

fast asleep, and snoring, but sitting upright in his chair. Poking out of his pocket was a key, and cradled in his arms was Elf Girl's bow.

'The pig!' cried Elf Girl.

'Shh!' hushed Raven Boy. 'You'll wake him up!'

Elf Girl nodded, and they tiptoed over very carefully indeed.

At close range, his snoring was deafening, but Raven Boy reached out one hand and slowly pulled the key from Scrim's pocket.

He held it up, grinning at Elf Girl, who started to try and pull her bow from the captain's arms.

'No!' whispered Raven Boy as loud as he dared. 'No! Don't!'

Raven Boy could see Elf Girl wasn't going to stop, and hurried back out of the cabin, running over the captive girl.

Holding his breath, Raven Boy tried the key.

It fitted! Within moments, she was free. Rat jumped off her head and back into Raven Boy's pocket.

'Oh, thank you!' she said, happily.

'Right,' said Raven Boy. 'Let's get out of here. Help me lower that rowing boat, would you?'

He pointed at the pirate's jolly boat, which needed winding down on a winch to the sea.

They wound the handles as fast as they could, and the little boat was just about to touch the water, when suddenly they heard a noise like a rhinoceros sneezing. That was followed by shouts and the sound of running feet; pointy boots and pirate boots. Elf Girl emerged from the captain's cabin, closely followed by the captain himself, waving her bow and looking furious.

'Go!' shouted Elf Girl. 'Go! Into the boat!'

Raven Boy didn't need telling twice, and clambered into the boat in a flash. He could hear the other pirates waking up and more angry shouting and fuss.

He grabbed the oars and though he didn't really know what he was doing, he managed to start the boat moving, just as Elf Girl reached the railings, and flung herself into the boat, where she landed with a bump.

'Where's that girl you were so keen on rescuing?' she asked.

Raven Boy shrugged, then Rat squeaked loudly, and they both saw her.

'Look!'

The girl was standing on the rail of the deck, and it looked as if she was about to be grabbed by a dozen pirates, when she dived neatly off the side of the ship and into the water, barely making a splash.

'Wow!' said Raven Boy. 'Cool!'

'Shut up and row, Raven Face,' said Elf Girl. 'They're coming!'

'Elf Girl, are you jealous?' asked Raven Boy.

She was, it was true, and it was also true that the pirates were coming after them, but were so sleepy that they didn't really know what was going on.

They were running around in all directions, the captain was waving the bow above his head shouting 'Garr!', and a couple of pigs leapt from the ship into the water.

'Row!' cried Elf Girl, and Raven Boy did his best. After a while, Elf Girl pointed out he was facing the wrong way, and then they took one oar each, and soon put some distance between the pirate ship and themselves.

'Where's that girl gone?' shouted Raven Boy.

'Here I am!' she said, and popped her head over the back end of the boat.

She turned and laughed at the pirates, watching as one of them tripped over a pig and fell overboard.

'Quick,' cried Raven Boy, as even Elf Girl made a space for her. 'Get into the boat and let's get out of here. We won't have to go far and they won't be able to see us in the dark.'

'Thanks,' said the girl, 'but I'm happier in the water. It was nice of you to rescue me, by the way. My name's Molo. What's yours?'

'That's a funny name,' said Raven Boy.

'He's called Raven Boy and I'm Elf Girl,' said Elf Girl.

'And you think my name's funny?' said Molo. 'Anyway, thank you Raven Boy, thank you Elf Girl. Without you I'd have been sold for sure.'

'And so would we,' said Elf Girl. 'But not for as much as you. Why are you worth so much more than us anyway?'

Molo shrugged.

'Listen, I'm going now.'

'You're going? But where? There's nowhere to go.'

'Yes there is,' Molo said, 'but if I were you, I'd row that way.'

She pointed towards the moon.

'Don't go that way either,' she added, pointing north. 'That's the way to Blackheart Isle. And keep well away from Scream Sea too.'

She bobbed about in the water, pointing this way and that.

'But I want you to know,' she went
on, 'that if you ever need any help, just blow
through this, and I'll come. With my friends.'

She fished around her
neck and pulled a tiny silvery
chain off, handing it to Raven
Boy. On it was a small shell with
a hole through it. It sparkled
like shimmering fish scales in
the starlight. Raven Boy put it to
his lips.

'Don't!' cried Molo. 'Only
once, when you need it. And
we'll come.'

'What do you mean?'
asked Raven Boy, sounding confused.

'Who'll come?' asked Elf Girl, feeling
just as puzzled.

'We will!' cried Molo, laughing, and with
that, she ducked away from the boat, taking a
swoop underwater, and then, as she surfaced
and ducked under again, they saw something
that made them both stop rowing and their
mouths fall open.

'Did you see that?' asked Raven Boy.

'No, I didn't,' said Elf Girl. 'No way.'

'You did! I know you did,' said Raven Boy.

'Yes, all right,' said Elf Girl. 'I did see it, but I must be crazy in the head.'

Raven Boy said nothing, because just then, they got a last glimpse of Molo as she swam away. There, where her legs should have been, they caught sight of a long and glistening fish's tail.

'Mermaid,' whispered Raven Boy.

'Wow,' whispered Elf Girl.

Raven Boy looked at the shell whistle, and tucked it in his pocket, next to Rat.

The shouts of angry pirates floated across the water.

'Come on, Elf Girl, we need to row some more.'

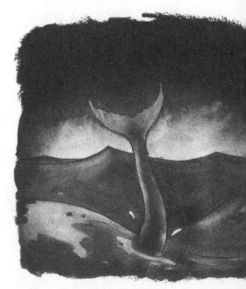

TEN

Raven Boy lives in the treetops, and once didn't touch the ground for over a year, just to see if he could.

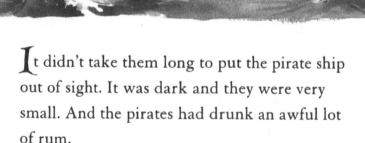

It didn't take them long to put the pirate ship out of sight. It was dark and they were very small. And the pirates had drunk an awful lot of rum.

'So that's why she was worth so much,' said Elf Girl, as they kept rowing. 'She was a mermaid. She didn't have a tail when she was on the ship though.'

'Maybe because she was out of the water.

She turned into a normal girl. But that explains where she came from too,' said Raven Boy. 'No land around here; they must have pulled her out of the sea.'

'Well, it was very foolish of her to get caught,' said Elf Girl.

'You could say the same about us,' said Raven Boy.

They rowed on in silence for a while.

'I've lost my bow,' said Elf Girl sadly.

'I know,' said Raven Boy. 'Maybe it's for the best?'

Elf Girl stopped rowing and glared at him.

'What's that supposed to mean?'

'I just mean it didn't always do what you wanted it to. We might have had an accident one day with it. A serious accident.'

'And without it we'd both be troll food by now, wouldn't we?'

'I suppose so,' said Raven Boy, grudgingly.

'Which way are we rowing, anyway?' asked Elf Girl.

'Towards the moon,' said Raven Boy.

'What, just because Molo said so?'

'Yes, just because Molo said so,' said Raven Boy. 'Do you have any better ideas? And anyway, she told us not to head north, which must be over there, if the moon's that way.'

He pointed with his chin.

'But we don't know what's out there,' said Elf Girl. 'She doesn't need land! She's a fish! Maybe she doesn't know we need to find land. And then water, and food.'

'I think she was trying to help us,' said Raven Boy.

'You would,' said Elf Girl.

'And what's that supposed to mean?'

'Nothing,' said Elf Girl. 'You're just so nice to everyone. All the time. And look where it gets us! Always in trouble.'

Raven Boy ignored her. He could tell she was just tired and grumpy.

'Elf Girl,' he said, gently, 'you're nice too. I know you are. You're just scared, that's all.'

'Am not!' snapped Elf Girl, and Raven Boy decided to keep his mouth closed for a while.

They rowed on, and on, and finally, the sun began to come up.

When it did, they saw that they were alone on the wide, wide sea, and that there was not a single other thing in sight.

'If there was even a seagull I could talk

to . . . ' said Raven Boy. But there was no more a seagull in the air than a horse.

'Oh, Raven Boy,' said Elf Girl. 'Now which way do we go? The moon's gone! Look!'

'Maybe we should blow Molo's whistle. Get her help.'

Raven Boy pulled the shell from his pocket and looked at it.

'I don't think she meant us to use it for something as simple as being lost. I think it's for something more serious.'

'If we never get off this ocean, that will be pretty serious!' cried Elf Girl. She looked upset.

'Don't panic,' said Raven Boy, at which Rat poked his head up and squeaked loudly.

'That includes you, Rat,' said Raven Boy, but as the day wore on, they gave up rowing and lay in the boat, just drifting on the ocean.

It began to get hot, very hot, and there was no shelter in the boat, nor anything to drink. They tried to rest, and soon, with the rocking of the boat and the heat of the sun, they fell asleep.

It was much later when they woke, and

they woke because the boat was rocking much harder.

Raven Boy sat up.

The day had changed. The sun had hidden itself behind huge banks of clouds. There was a cold wind, and as Elf Girl sat up, rubbing her eyes, the first drops of rain splashed onto the planks of the boat.

A large wave lifted it up into the air, and then dropped it down again. The rain began to fall properly, and lightning flashed across the horizon.

'Oh, Elf Girl,' said Raven Boy. 'I think there's going to be a storm!'

'You think?' cried Elf Girl, and as she did, another massive wave rocked the boat from side to side, and the next one dumped a bathtub-full of water onto them.

Rat squeaked and hid deep inside Raven Boy's pocket, and then another wave swamped them, as the wind hit the boat and the rain lashed down and down.

'Oh!' wailed Elf Girl. 'Raven Boy! We'll be drowned.'

Raven Boy swallowed hard.

'Help me! Turn the nose of the boat into the waves!'

But it was no good, and in a few seconds, the waves tossed the boat right up, turned it over, and sent them sprawling into the cold, wild water.

Eleven

**Mermaids aren't scared to live in the
Scream Sea. They're so fast they can
outswim the biggest beastie.**

Raven Boy woke up.

That was the first surprising thing,
because the last thing he remembered was
plunging underwater for the hundredth time,
thinking he was about to drown, along with Elf
Girl and Rat.

He blinked.

The second surprising thing was that he
was dry. Bone dry. A little too warm, if anything.

And thirdly, he was sitting on a sandy beach.

He blinked again, like a bird, and turned to see Elf Girl looking at him.

She blinked like an Elf Girl.

'Well, that was lucky,' she said.

Rat squeaked from Raven Boy's other side, and then hopped up onto his head. Just to say hello.

'Where are we?' asked Raven Boy.

'On an island, I think.'

'Not Blackheart Isle?'

'No, I don't think so,' said Elf Girl. 'It looks too small for that.'

Raven Boy stood up and looked about.

There was the sea, still wild and rough, and Raven Boy gasped as he saw the waves were almost red in colour.

'Look! It must be the waters of Scream Sea,' he said.

Behind him was a small island, small enough to almost see all around. The middle of the island was covered in a jungle of sinister-looking trees.

'Let's explore,' said Raven Boy. So they

did, setting off along the beach, and half an hour later, they found their own footprints again.

'It's an island!' said Raven Boy.

Elf Girl groaned. 'We knew that!'

'Anyway,' said Raven Boy, 'what are we going to do? We've been washed up on a desert island; we could be anywhere!'

'Maybe it's time to blow Molo's whistle now.'

'No, I feel sure that's for something more serious.'

'More serious! What could be more serious than being marooned on a desert island?'

'Look, we ought to have another look around before we panic. Maybe someone lives here – maybe someone can help us.'

'Where?' cried Elf Girl. 'We've just walked all around it.'

'Yes,' said Raven Boy. 'But we haven't tried in there.'

He nodded at the jungle that covered the middle of the island.

'At least, I might find an animal to talk to, work out where we are and how to get away.'

'And how are we going to get away? Ask a big parrot to carry us?'

'There's no need to be sarcastic,' said Raven Boy. 'Maybe we can build a raft! There are trees, after all!'

Elf Girl rolled her eyes, but Raven Boy ignored her and set off up the beach, towards the trees. Rat scampered along after him, excited to be back on land, with lots of new things to sniff.

Elf Girl rolled her eyes again and then

felt it was a waste because no one was there to see it, and trudged after the other two.

They hadn't got far.

The trees were packed so tightly together that it was difficult to force a way through.

'This is stupid,' moaned Elf Girl.

'Elf Girl,' said Raven Boy, 'you are not being very positive today. Maybe you could say nothing, if you can't say anything helpful.'

Elf Girl muttered something that he didn't hear.

'Pardon?' he asked.

'Nothing,' said Elf Girl. 'You're right. It's just that we're stuck on this island, and I've lost my bow and then there's the Goblin King thing.'

'What?' asked Raven Boy, who'd been crashing through a branch and hadn't heard.

'The Goblin King! We still don't know what to do, or where to go, or anything.'

Raven Boy agreed, but he didn't want to upset her any more, so he just nodded, and pushed on into the jungle.

'We might find some fruit to eat,' he said. 'That would be a start.'

And then, they stumbled out from the trees and found themselves in a clearing.

There, stood a funny little shack.

'You were saying?' asked Raven Boy, feeling pleased with himself.

Elf Girl sighed.

'All right, Smart Beak, you win. Let's have a look.'

Raven Boy nodded.

'But Raven Boy! Be careful! It could be dangerous.'

He nodded again.

As it turned out, Elf Girl was, as so often, right.

TWELVE

**Rat loves sitting on Raven Boy's head,
because it makes him feel not so little
for a while.**

The shack had a single room, and even that
had only two walls and a roof. What kept the
roof from falling down was a wooden post in
the corner where the two missing walls would
have met.

It had a wooden floor and even a tatty
piece of carpet on it, and standing on the floor
was a very old and beaten-up armchair, a table,
and a bed pushed against one of the walls. One

of the actual walls. There were a few cupboards and shelves, and all sorts of odd things, all of which looked very old and raggedy. There was even an oil painting, a portrait of a strange-looking man, hanging on one of the walls.

It looked as though no one had been there for years.

'Wow,' said Elf Girl. 'What a weird place!'

They found lots of books, maps, charts, and peculiar objects that they didn't even know the names of, pencils, more books, and more stuff that made no sense at all.

They sat on the carpet, staring in different directions, both feeling a little sulky.

Rat scuttled under the bed, fearing that they were about to start arguing again.

And none of them saw the footprints walking towards the shack, across the sand. Just footprints, appearing one by one, with nothing else attached.

'You smell.'

'I do not!' cried Raven Boy and Elf Girl, whirling round to look at each other.

'Why did you say that?' they both said together.

'What?' they both said.

'What are you doing?' asked Raven Boy.

'Stop being silly,' said Elf Girl.

They turned away to sulk again.

'You still smell.'

They both turned and glared at each other.

'I do not!' they both said, and then,
'Stop it!'

'Raven Boy . . . '

'Elf Girl . . . '

They glared at each other, and turned away once more.

'Smell-y!'

And with that they both jumped on each other, kicking and scratching and generally being naughty.

And they would have gone on, except a coconut fell on their heads.

'Ow!' said Raven Boy, rubbing his bird hair.

Another coconut fell on Elf Girl.

'Eee!' she wailed.

They looked up, and saw that there wasn't a tree above their heads.

'Where did that come from?' asked Raven Boy, too puzzled to feel hurt now.

'I don't—' began Elf Girl, but she didn't finish, because another coconut came hurtling at them.

'Ow! That really hurt,' moaned Raven Boy, rubbing his backside.

Suddenly the coconuts came thick and fast, and they began to try to dodge them, and work out where they were coming from at the same time.

'Look!' cried Elf Girl. She ducked a flying coconut and pointed to the side of the shack, where there was a whole pile of coconuts, which appeared to be picking themselves up and throwing themselves through thin air.

'Magic coconuts!' shrieked Elf Girl.

'Haunted, you mean!' wailed Raven Boy, as another nut clipped his ear.

The coconuts kept flying, and then suddenly there was the sound of someone sneezing loudly, and the next second, a man appeared from nowhere, holding a coconut in each hand.

'Ooh!' shouted Elf Girl. 'Get him!'

'Yes,' said Raven Boy, who was really mad at being hit by so many coconuts. 'Get him!'

They charged the man, and pinned him to the ground. He was not that big and not that strong either, and Elf Girl and Raven Boy had no trouble holding him down, though Rat sat on his face just to make sure. There was something very odd about him, though. His skin seemed to be made of sand.

'I'm sorry,' he said, 'please don't hurt me!

I won't tell anyone you're here; just leave me alone.'

'What do you mean?' asked Raven Boy.

'Please let me up. I won't do anything, I promise.'

'Why do you keep saying that?' asked Elf Girl.

They let him up, because he was sniffing a lot by now and they had started to feel sorry for him.

'Because if the other pirates come here and know you've been here they'll be awfully mad.'

'Other pirates?' asked Raven Boy.

'Yes, the other pirates.'

The man looked puzzled. He had rather crazy eyes and a long beard, which made him look even more strange.

'You are pirates, aren't you?' he said.

'No,' said Elf Girl. 'We're not. I'm Elf Girl and this is Raven Boy.'

Rat squeaked.

'Oh yes, and that's Rat.'

'Pleased to meet you,' said the man. Then added suspiciously, 'Are you sure you aren't pirates?'

'Totally sure,' explained Raven Boy. 'We've just escaped from pirates, and then lost our boat in a storm. Then we washed up here.'

'Oh,' said the old man.

'And who are you, anyway? You haven't introduced yourself.'

'Oh, yes,' said the man. 'My name's Mervin.'

'May I ask you a personal question?' asked Raven Boy.

Mervin glared at him.

'It depends.'

Raven Boy ignored that answer and plunged straight in with the thing that had been bothering him.

'Are you aware you seem to be covered

in sand?'

Mervin exploded. Well, he didn't, but he did exclaim very loudly.

'Of course I'm covered in sand! In fact, I'm made of sand! I wouldn't be much of a Sandman if I wasn't, would I?'

'A Sandman?' cried Elf Girl and Raven Boy together, and even Rat squeaked. 'You're made of sand? That's not possible!'

'Of course it is,' said Mervin, huffily. 'You can be made of anything when you're magical.'

'You can do magic?'

'Of course I can,' said Mervin proudly. 'That's how we fly round the world putting little children to sleep every night.'

Then he looked sad.

'Only I'm not very good any more,' he said. 'I've forgotten almost everything.'

'But you made yourself invisible!'

'Yes, but that's all I can do. That and make food. I've forgotten how to do anything else. And even the invisibility thing is pretty hopeless. It wears off when you sneeze.'

'When you sneeze?' asked Elf Girl, but

Raven Boy had other things on his mind.

'Did you say make food?' he asked, his eyes widening.

'Yes,' said Mervin. 'Would you like some?'

And Raven Boy and Elf Girl nodded so hard their heads nearly fell off.

Thirteen

Raven Boy is always discovering new things about Elf Girl. Only yesterday he found out that she can't eat raisins. They give her green spots.

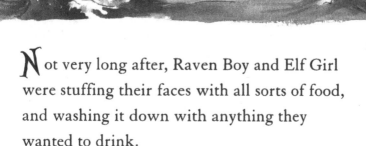

Not very long after, Raven Boy and Elf Girl were stuffing their faces with all sorts of food, and washing it down with anything they wanted to drink.

It seemed that Mervin the Sandman was still very good at making food, and he could make whatever they asked for, only more delicious than they thought possible.

'I get lots of practice with food magic,'

the magician explained. 'There's not much
else to do here. Only make food, and avoid the
pirates when they come to bury their treasure.'

'Captain Scrim?' asked Elf Girl, her
mouth full of bread roll and raspberry jam.

Mervin laughed.

'Ha! Him! I'm not scared of him! He's
just a nimby-pimby, namby-pamby, flimsy-
wimsy, ittle-wittle . . . '

'Yes, we get the idea,' interrupted Raven
Boy. 'But are you sure you mean Captain

Scrim? The captain of the *Naughty Porpoise*? He was about to sell us as slaves!'

'Ha!' cried Mervin again. 'That's nothing. Being sold as slaves would be a luxury compared to what Blackblood would do to you.'

'Blackblood?' cried Elf Girl and Raven Boy together, their eyes widening, and their mouths opening. Crumpet crumbs fell out and onto the tatty carpet, and Rat pounced on them.

'Yes!' Mervin said, 'Captain Blackblood. He's a real pirate!'

'But Captain Scrim was going to pull our toes off.'

'A picnic!' cried Mervin, 'compared with what Blackblood would do to you. A picnic, you hear?'

Raven Boy and Elf Girl stopped eating.

'So who is Captain Blackblood?' they asked, looking around nervously as if he might appear at any minute.

'He pirates the seas to the east of here. From here, all the way east to the mainland, the ocean is known as the Scream Sea.'

'I knew it!' cried Raven Boy. 'The red waves!'

Mervin nodded.

'Red waves is nothing. The sea is full of monsters too. Great beasts from the deep, with the wrong number of legs and too many eyes. Most people, most normal people, are too scared to sail on Scream Sea. And the few that do have to face up to one more thing: Captain Blackblood and the crew of the *Sea Dragon*. They're the ones to be scared of. Not Captain Scrim and his bunch of daisies!'

'But, but,' said Raven Boy, 'but, does Captain Blackblood come here? Will he be coming here soon?'

'I have no idea,' said Mervin. 'They come every now and again, and bury their treasure. And then they come back other times, when they're ready to sell whatever they have. It's like a bank, here, on the island. They put their stuff in the sand, and they dig it up again when they need it.'

'And you just avoid them? Don't they know about your little hut here?'

'Oh yes, but they think it's haunted. I make myself invisible and throw some things around, and they keep well away.'

'Aren't you scared of sneezing?'

Mervin glared at Elf Girl.

'Enjoying your food, are you?'

'Oh yes, sorry. It's very nice, thank you.'

'You're a very good magician,' added Raven Boy. 'In fact, you're so good, why do you stay here? It can't be much fun. Can't you make a magic boat and sail away?'

Mervin made a cup of tea appear, in thin air, caught it, and took a sip.

'I don't want to.'

'But you're here all alone. Are there other people like you? Other Sandmen?'

'Yes, lots of them, and they can stay where they are, thanks very much. That's why I came here.'

'Why?' asked Elf Girl.

'To get away from them! I'm not like other Sandmen. I like peace and quiet and they . . . Oh, well, if you ever met them, you'd see! Talking all the time. It was unbearable. So I came here for a nice rest, and I liked it so much, I stayed.'

'Aren't you lonely?'

'Not at all! I like it here. Nobody bothers me. Usually,' he added, staring at the pair of them.

'We don't want to intrude,' said Elf Girl. 'We'd be very happy to leave. We have to! We're on an important quest, you see.'

'Really?' asked Mervin, taking another sip of tea. His eyes narrowed slightly.

'Yes, we're going to save the world from the Goblin King!'

Mervin spluttered and sprayed tea all over Raven Boy and Elf Girl.

FOURTEEN

Most Sandmen aren't very interested in cooking, which Mervin thinks is a terrible shame when you can make anything you like.

'The Goblin King?' said Mervin again. 'You're going to fight the Goblin King?'

'Yes,' said Raven Boy. 'Have you heard of him?'

Mervin the Sandman rolled his eyes.

'You're mad!' he said. 'It was nice meeting you. I expect you'll be dead very soon so it's probably not worth me making you any more food.'

'Dead?' wailed Elf Girl.

'Don't you know how deadly the Goblin King is? Just his little toe is scarier than Captain Blackblood and all of his crew put together. If you found all the scary monsters in the Scream Sea and added them all up, they'd be about as scary as one of the Goblin King's nostrils!'

Raven Boy and Elf Girl looked each other.

'We've heard he's bad . . . ' began Elf Girl.

'Bad! *Bad*?' cried Mervin. 'Ha!'

Then he tapped the side of his head with one long forefinger.

'You're nuts!'

'But we have to!' cried Raven Boy. 'We have to save the world. He's trying to destroy our forest. He sent an ogre to pull up all the trees. We defeated him!'

Mervin stopped tapping his head.

'You did?'

He looked quite impressed.

'Yes, and we climbed the Monster Mountains. Only now we're stuck.'

'Yes, you are. On the edge of Scream Sea.'

Raven Boy and Elf Girl looked very sad.

'Maybe you're right,' said Raven Boy. 'Maybe we should give up and go home. If we could! How can we even get off this island?'

Rat squeaked and Raven Boy picked him up and stroked him.

'I know, Rat,' he said. 'I know you want to go home.'

'But we can't!' cried Elf Girl. 'We've come so far and anyway, we know how to defeat the Goblin King!'

'You do?' asked Mervin.

'Sort of,' Elf Girl said. 'Raven Boy found out that in order to defeat him, we need something called the Singing Sword, and something called the Tears of the Moon.'

'Only we don't know what they are,' said Raven Boy.

'The Singing Sword is

a sword,' said Mervin. 'That sings. It's pretty obvious really.'

'Well, we didn't know,' said Raven Boy, grumpily. 'What about the Tears of the Moon?'

'I . . . er . . . ' said Mervin. 'I don't know. But I do know where to find them.'

'You do?' asked Elf Girl.

'Yes,' said Mervin. 'You see, whenever the pirates come and bury their treasure here, I make myself invisible and listen to their stories, and hear what they're talking about and so on.'

'And you've heard about the Sword, and the Tears?'

'Oh yes,' said Mervin. 'Many times. You see, of all the treasures the pirates get, none of them are as precious as the Singing Sword, or the Tears of the Moon. That's what they say. Only they're too scared to go and find them.'

'Captain Blackblood is too scared?' asked Raven Boy, his eyes wide with fear.

Mervin nodded slowly.

'Yes, you see, to get the Singing Sword, and the Tears of the Moon, you would have to go to the very middle of the Dread Desert.'

'The Dread Desert?'

'Do you have to repeat everything I say?' asked Mervin.

'Sorry,' said Raven Boy.

'Anyway, yes, the Dread Desert. Full of spooky spirits and strange happenings. It's huge. Vast. There's nothing to drink, and it's as hot as the sun. No one's ever come back alive!'

Elf Girl gulped.

'How do you know all this, anyway?' she asked.

'It's where I come from,' Mervin explained. 'Where us sandpeople live. The Dread Desert.'

'EEP,' said Raven Boy. Then he stood up. 'We have to try. We have to try anyway. We can't just let the Goblin King take over the world. Destroy the forests, and turn the people into slaves. No!'

'But Raven Boy,' asked Elf Girl, 'how are we going to get off this island?'

Mervin stood up.

'If you're determined to go,' he said, 'I can help you.'

Raven Boy and Elf Girl sat up straight.

'Yes, all we have to do is wait until next time Captain Blackblood and his crew arrive to dig up some treasure. After they've done that they usually head east over Scream Sea and go and spend all their money in a port on the mainland. A port called Waterspout.'

'So how does that help us?' asked Raven Boy. 'You've already told us he's the most fearsome pirate on the sea. We can't exactly ask him for a ride, can we?'

'No,' agreed Mervin. 'Nor can you just stow away on his ship, because if he found you, which he certainly would, he would barbecue you before the day was out.'

'EEP,' said Raven Boy again.

'Stop saying that,' said Elf Girl. She looked hard at Mervin. 'So what's your plan?'

'My plan,' said Mervin, 'is quite simply to make you both invisible. Then next time Blackblood and his crew show up, all you need to do is swim over to the ship, find somewhere out of the way to hide, and wait till you get to Waterspout.'

'That could work!' cried Raven Boy.

'And you could make Rat invisible too?' asked Elf Girl.

'Yes, of course. And even better than that,' Mervin went on, 'I can make some food for your journey, and make that invisible too. I have to say it makes eating a little messy, but you'll get the hang of it.'

'Hooray!' cried Raven Boy.

Elf Girl didn't look so certain, but she smiled anyway.

'There's just one thing,' said Mervin, very seriously.

'Which is?' asked Elf Girl.

'Which is this. You have to be very careful not to sneeze. If you do . . . '

Elf Girl closed her eyes.

Raven Boy gulped again.

'Oh, nuts,' he said, 'I'd forgotten that.'

'But come on, how often do you sneeze?' asked Mervin brightly. 'Really? I'm sure you'll be fine. Just stay away from the ship's pepperpots, eh?'

FIFTEEN

Elf Girl has travelled much more than Raven Boy. She even went on a beach holiday once, but didn't like what the sand did to her shoes.

Raven Boy and Elf Girl were sick of waiting for Captain Blackblood to arrive. It was awful.

They knew they needed him to come so they could get off the island, but the longer they waited, the more scared they got.

With every day that passed, Mervin would make them food, and they would spend their days staring at the red waves of Scream Sea or, in Raven Boy's case, climbing the trees in the jungle, just to check he hadn't forgotten how to.

'Which is worse?' asked Elf Girl one day. They were strolling on the beach, looking out to sea. Rat was tired and taking a free ride on Raven Boy's head. 'If Captain Blackblood never comes, and we're stuck here for ever, or if he does, and we have to sneak onto his ship?'

Raven Boy put his head on one side.

'That's a tough question,' he said. 'The more I hear about Blackblood from Mervin, the worse he sounds! But we have to get off this island to save the world from the Goblin King.'

Elf Girl nodded.

'And anyway,' she said, ' it's good practice.'

'What is?' asked Raven Boy.

'Facing scarier and scarier enemies. That way, when we finally get to the Goblin King, he won't seem so bad.'

'I hope you're right about that.'

'Of course I am. I'm always right.'

'Usually,' said Raven Boy, laughing.

'What?' said Elf Girl.

Rat squeaked.

'Don't worry,' said Raven Boy. 'We're just joking. We're not actually going to have another fight.'

'Aren't we?' asked Elf Girl, but Rat ignored them and squeaked again, once, very loudly.

Raven Boy looked out to sea.

'He said he can . . . Oh! Look!'

Now they both saw what Rat had seen, because sailing into view over the horizon was a big ship. A big ship with coal-black sails.

'It must be Captain Blackblood!' Raven Boy gasped.

'Let's find Mervin! It's time to get invisible!'

They ran back up the beach and into the clearing.

Mervin had made a huge cake, several tiers high, and was just wishing up some cherries to put on the top.

'There!' he said, admiring his handiwork. 'Done!'

'Mervin!' cried Elf Girl. 'They're here! A ship's coming! We think it's the *Sea Dragon*.'

'Does it have black sails?'

Raven Boy and Elf Girl nodded.

'Yes, that's it,' said Mervin. 'Oh, bother. And I've just finished this cake.'

'Never mind the cake!' screamed Raven Boy. 'Make us invisible! Quick!'

'All in good time,' said Mervin. 'Won't you have a piece of birthday cake first?'

'Please make us invisible!' begged Raven Boy. 'And then we'll have as much cake as you like. We promise!'

Mervin thought for a moment.

'All right,' he said. 'Very well. Come on then, stand in front of me, here.'

'And Rat?' asked Raven Boy.

'And the rat too,' said Mervin. 'Now, just stand still, and here we go.'

Raven Boy and Elf Girl were panicking so much they didn't even see what it was Mervin did to turn them invisible. He didn't have a magic wand, and they didn't even hear him say any magic words but, next thing they knew, they'd vanished.

'Elf Girl!' said Raven Boy excitedly, 'I can't see you! You've gone!'

'I'm right here,' she said, 'but so have you! Pouf! Just like that!'

'Rat? Are you there?'

From Raven Boy's head, Rat squeaked.

'Just stay on my head, okay? I don't want to step on you.'

Rat squeaked again, and dug his claws into Raven Boy's spiky hair.

'Now,' said Mervin, 'won't you have a piece of cake?'

'But I can still see you,' said Elf Girl. 'And the cake. Won't you make everything invisible first? So we can stop worrying about the pirates!'

Mervin sighed.

'Very well,' he said at last, and then he vanished and, a moment later, so did his cake.

'It looked so pretty,' he said. 'It's a shame not to see it. Well, anyway, let me cut you a slice and then you can sing me happy birthday.'

'Sing?' cried Raven Boy.

'Yes, sing!' said Mervin. 'It's my birthday. You do want to sing to me, don't you? After I've been so helpful, and— '

'Yes, yes,' said Raven Boy, quickly. 'Just give me some cake and let's get on with it.'

So they did.

They all had cake and Raven Boy and Elf Girl sang happy birthday to Mervin, and then he seemed happier. Even Rat joined in.

No sooner had they finished than they heard shouts down on the beach.

'Blackblood!' cried Elf Girl.

'Shh!' hissed Raven Boy.

'Come on,' said Mervin. 'Let's go down and see what they're up to. Now, I've made a nice invisible packed lunch for you. There's enough for a few days, if you're careful. Here you are.'

'Where?' said Raven Boy.

'Here!' said Mervin. 'Just take it from me.'

'But I can't see you! Or it!'

'Oh, Raven Boy,' said Elf Girl, 'stop being so silly. Just use the sound of his voice. And feel for it. Here!'

She turned to where she thought Mervin was, just as Raven Boy tried again.

They bumped into each other and Elf Girl fell on her bottom.

'Oh,' she said.

'What?'

'Mervin. I'm so sorry. I think I've just sat on your birthday cake.'

SIXTEEN

Mervin the Sandman can't remember the spell that would repair the walls of his hut. He once tried to use cake to do it, but the seagulls ate it.

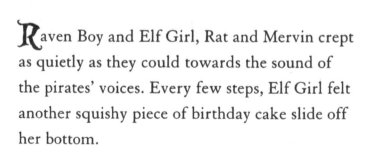

Raven Boy and Elf Girl, Rat and Mervin crept as quietly as they could towards the sound of the pirates' voices. Every few steps, Elf Girl felt another squishy piece of birthday cake slide off her bottom.

'I'm going to smell of chocolate cake for days,' she moaned.

'Shh!' said Raven Boy, 'we're nearly there. Look!'

There, beyond the edge of the trees, were the pirates. They were digging at the top of the beach, underneath a tall coconut tree.

'Where's Blackblood?' whispered
Raven Boy.

'There!' said Mervin. 'In the black jacket.'

'What, behind that little pirate?'

'He *is* the little pirate,' whispered Mervin.

'What? He doesn't look so scary!'

'Trust me!' said Mervin. 'The little ones
are the mean ones! He's as vicious and nasty as
a short-tempered snake. Believe me!'

Raven Boy looked again. Blackblood was very, very short, and although he had a long and silly moustache, he didn't look that scary. After all the waiting, they'd expected to see someone five metres tall with hands the size of dogs, and teeth made of chisels.

'You're in luck!' whispered Mervin. 'They're digging something up, not burying something. That means they'll be going straight to Waterspout to spend some money. It should only take a couple of days to cross Scream Sea.'

'Good!' said Raven Boy.

'Assuming you're not eaten by sea monsters first, of course,' Mervin added.

Raven Boy and Elf Girl swallowed.

'Now's your chance!' hissed Mervin. 'You can wade out halfway to the *Sea Dragon*, then swim to the anchor and climb up the anchor chain. Are you any good at climbing?'

'Two of us are,' said Elf Girl, sounding worried.

'We'll help you,' said Raven Boy.

Rat squeaked.

'He says he doesn't want

to get his fur wet swimming,' said Raven Boy.

'Rat can stay on your head, yes?' said Elf Girl. 'So come on!'

'Mervin, thank you for everything. How can we repay you?'

'Just don't tell anyone I'm here,' he said. 'And give the Goblin King one for me, eh? Now go on, goodbye.'

'Goodbye, Mervin!'

They crept down to the water, scared in case the pirates saw their footsteps appearing in the sand, but they were all too busy waiting to dig their treasure up.

They reached the water's edge, and swam out to the ship.

'Elf Girl, are you there?'

'I'm here! I'm right here!'

'Can you climb the anchor chain?'

'I'll have to!' she cried.

'Go on! We'll wait!'

She did. Or at least, she tried to.

Raven Boy saw wet marks appearing on the chain, as her hands grabbed hold of it, and then moved a little higher, but then there was

a big splash in the water beside him, and the
sound of spluttering a moment later.

'Try again,' said Raven Boy, glancing
nervously towards the beach.

'It's hard holding the food parcel too,'
said Elf Girl.

'I'll take that,' said Raven Boy. 'Now try again!'

And she did, but a few moments later, there was a big splash in the water, and more spluttering.

'It's no good,' said Elf Girl. 'I can't do it!'

'You have to! Try again!'

So she did, and for the third time, she fell back into the salty water.

'Listen,' said Raven Boy. 'I'll go up first, and find a rope. Then you tie it round you and I'll try and pull you while you climb.'

'Okay,' said Elf Girl, miserably. 'But hurry, I'm getting tired!'

Raven Boy climbed up the chain in double-quick time, and Rat leaped from his head, and they scurried around the deck of the pirate ship, quickly finding a spare rope, which they lowered to Elf Girl.

'Tie it round your waist!' cried Raven Boy.

He looked at the beach, and with his heart in his mouth, saw that the pirates had finished digging, and were returning to the ship.

'Quickly!' he called to Elf Girl.

Though he couldn't see her, he suddenly felt a weight at the end of the rope, and he pulled as hard as he could, while she climbed the chain.

Suddenly, the rope went slack, and there was a thump on the deck in front of him.

'Ow!' said Elf Girl.

'Never mind that!' cried Raven Boy. 'They'll be here any second! Quick! We have to find a place to hide.'

'Have you got our food?' wailed Elf Girl.

'Oh! Good point! I put it down here somewhere . . . '

Raven Boy began feeling about on the deck for the food parcels.

Rat began to squeak.

'Rat's found it!' cried Raven Boy. 'Only I don't know where he is!'

Rat squeaked again.

'There's no time!' hissed Elf Girl. 'They're here!'

The pirates were already climbing a rope ladder from their long boat.

'Come on!' whispered Raven Boy. 'Up to

the crow's nest!'

Of course, Raven Boy was up the rigging
of the ship and into the crow's nest in a few
seconds, and Rat with him, but it took Elf Girl
a couple of minutes to manage the same climb.

'Can we please stop climbing everywhere?'
she whispered.

'I thought it would be the safest place
for now,' Raven Boy whispered
back. 'Look! The deck's swarming
with pirates.'

They peered down from the crow's nest, at the top of the main mast, and watched the pirates hauling their treasure up and dancing about on deck, full of glee.

Captain Blackblood stood, staring at something. He had a puzzled look on his face and was ignoring the commotion his pirates were making.

'He's seen our footprints!'

'Oh no!'

Blackblood was about to take a closer look at the footprints on the deck, when one of his men tripped over something. Something invisible.

'Our food!' hissed Elf Girl.

The pirate turned and saw one of his shipmates laughing at him.

'Trip me up, would ya?' said the pirate who'd fallen, and jumped to his feet, squaring up to the other one.

'You tripped yourself, you stupid ninny.'

'Why you . . . '

Seconds later, there was a crazy pirate brawl in full swing, and Blackblood was barking at his men to stop.

'Raven Boy . . . ' said Elf Girl.

'I know,' said Raven Boy. 'We have to get that food back, before they find it. And us!'

SEVENTEEN

**Elf Girl is convinced her magic bow has a
mind of its own. Just when she thinks
she has it figured out, it does
something different.**

The pirates stopped fighting when Blackblood
shouted at them, and Raven Boy and Elf Girl
could see just how mean and scary a pirate
captain he was.

He soon had the whole crew busy getting
the ship underway, and Raven Boy, Elf Girl
and Rat watched wistfully as they left the little
island behind them, and Mervin with it.

Soon they were far out to sea, with no

sign of land once more. More than that, they were now sailing on Scream Sea, and with it, there was every chance of having their faces sucked off by a sea monster at any time, day or night.

They soon realised that it had actually been quite nice not being able to save the world for a while, and sitting on the beach every day and waiting for Mervin to make whatever they wanted to eat.

Thinking about food, they stared down to the deck, somewhere upon which were their two packed lunches.

'Where did we leave them?' Raven Boy asked Rat, and Rat squeaked.

'By the big wheel thing,' Raven Boy explained to Elf Girl.

'But it's so busy down there!' whispered Elf Girl. 'We're sure to get caught!'

'Maybe we should wait till dark,' said Raven Boy.

'What difference will that make?' asked Elf Girl. 'We're invisible.'

'Yes, but most of the pirates will go to

bed, won't they? We'd be less likely to bump into one.'

'We can't leave it that long! They might find our invisible food, accidentally!'

'It's funny being invisible, isn't it?' said Raven Boy.

'Raven Boy! Concentrate! Are we going to get this food now, or not?'

In the end, they did. Or rather, Raven Boy decided to go down to the deck and find it. It made more sense for only one of them to go, and he was better at climbing, after all.

Elf Girl and Rat watched nervously from the crow's nest, but of course they couldn't see him, and didn't even know how close several of the pirates came to bumping into Raven Boy.

Raven Boy was so light on the rigging, they didn't notice anything at all until suddenly he said, 'I'm back!' and dropped two parcels of invisible food at their feet.

Eating invisible food turned out to be quite hard. For a start, it was hard to work out what they were eating.

'I think this is jelly,' said Elf Girl.

'Jelly?' asked Raven Boy. 'What's that?'

'What a sheltered life you've led,' said Elf Girl, and tried to feed Raven Boy a handful of it, which turned out, when both they and the jelly were invisible, to be very messy indeed.

'That was a silly thing to pack,' said Elf Girl. 'What's wrong with a cucumber sandwich?'

As it happened, there were some nice sandwiches, but even eating sandwiches was hard when they couldn't see their hands, or their mouths, for that matter.

When they'd finished, there was possibly more food on the floor of the crow's nest than in their tummies, but they didn't know that and they felt a lot better, and as it got dark, they began to fall asleep.

'Raven Boy,' said Elf Girl, trying to get comfortable, 'my clothes are still wet.'

'Mine too,' said Raven Boy. 'It's cold.'

Although it had been a hot day, there was a cold wind up in the crow's nest and they shivered.

'Oh, well,' said Raven Boy. 'At least we're safe up here.'

'Just as long as none of them come up.'

'I don't think they will at night,' Raven Boy said.

'How do you know?'

'I don't,' he admitted. 'We'll have to sleep with one eye open.'

But in two blinks of an owl's eye, they were all fast asleep, with their eyes firmly shut.

They woke in the morning to the sound of shouting, and there was Blackblood on deck again, roaring at his crew.

Raven Boy and Elf Girl didn't know what had happened, but it seemed as if one of the pirates was in trouble for something, and he was getting told off with the greatest telling off in history.

When it was over, Elf Girl whispered to Raven Boy.

'You know something? I don't like that pirate one bit. The sooner we get off this ship the better.'

Raven Boy agreed.

But there was still no sign of land, and as the day wore on, they realised two things. First, they had already eaten all their food, apart from the bits they'd slept on accidentally, and secondly, they had nothing to drink.

By teatime, there was nothing for it.

'We're going to have to go down on deck,' said Elf Girl, 'find the ship's galley, and steal some food and drink.'

'EEP!' cheeped Raven Boy.

EIGHTEEN

Before Rat met Raven Boy he spent most days eating nuts and sleeping. He's happy he has someone to hang out with now.

They decided that they all had to go.

'We have to bring back as much food as we can,' said Elf Girl. 'We don't know how long we're going to be up here, after all.'

She sniffed a bit.

'Are you crying?' asked Raven Boy.

'No, I'm just a bit sniffly,' said Elf Girl. 'Sitting around in wet clothes all of yesterday. That's all.'

'Yes, I know what you mean,' agreed Raven Boy. 'Me too. So, it'll do us good to have a bit of exercise then. Come on!'

They peered over the side of the crow's nest, waiting till there were as few pirates around as possible. Then they scampered down the rigging, or Raven Boy and Rat scampered. Elf Girl still did not like climbing one bit, and though she did her best, she bumped into Raven Boy at the bottom, and stood on his toes.

'Ow!' he hissed.

'Sorry!' she whispered. 'Look, let's hold hands so we know where we both are.'

They did, and Rat sat on Raven Boy's head.

Rat sniffed the way to the galley, and very quietly squeaked directions to Raven Boy.

They crept along a corridor, and there were the kitchens. The cook was busy, throwing stuff around noisily as he made supper for the pirates.

Raven Boy picked up a loaf of bread, and froze.

'Elf Girl,' he hissed. 'We forgot something!'

'What?'

'This food's not invisible.'

Elf Girl muttered to herself.

'You've been listening to Blackblood too much,' said Raven Boy.

'Wait,' said Elf Girl.

The loaf of bread disappeared.

'What did you do?' asked Raven Boy, amazed.

'I put it up my dress.'

'You did what?'

'Shh! He'll hear you! Just be quiet and put as much food as you can inside your jacket.'

The cook was still banging away on the far side of the kitchen, so Raven Boy shoved a banana into his shirt, and it disappeared.

It was strange, watching things become invisible as they tucked them into their clothes, but very soon they could squeeze nothing more in, and Raven Boy was just putting a bottle in his jacket pocket when they decided it was time to leave.

Back along the corridor they crept, and started up the stairs to the deck.

Elf Girl was sniffing again.

'Shh!' whispered Raven Boy. 'Someone will hear you!'

'I can't help it,' said Elf Girl. 'I think I'm getting a cold.'

'Come on,' said Raven Boy, and they stepped out on deck again, where they had a shock.

It was swarming with pirates.

'Come on, you swabs!' Blackblood was screaming. 'Put your backs into it! This ship is a disgrace! I want to see it clean and tidy in twenty minutes, or I'll feed one of you to the beasties of Scream Sea!'

'Keep going!' whispered Raven Boy. 'Just be careful!'

They'd only taken a few more steps when Elf Girl stopped.

She sniffed.

'Elf Girl!' hissed Raven Boy. 'Don't!'

'I can't help it. I think . . . I think I'm going . . . to sneeze!'

'No!' whispered Raven Boy frantically. 'No!'

'I . . . ' said Elf Girl. 'I . . . '

'No!'

'Ah . . . ah . . . ' began Elf Girl.

Quickly, Raven Boy swung round and grabbed at where he guessed Elf Girl's nose might be, to stop her from sneezing.

But they'd made a lot of noise, and a circle of puzzled pirates had gathered around them, trying to work out where the talking was coming from.

'Shhh,' whispered Raven Boy, right into Elf Girl's ear.

And then Rat, who was sitting on Raven Boy's head, sneezed.

It was, in fact, only a little rodent sneeze, but the effect was the same. Mervin's spell wore off. One minute Rat was invisible, the next, it seemed to the pirates as if he'd suddenly appeared in mid-air, and was floating.

'Captain!' screeched the nearest pirate. 'Captain! There's a flying rat on board! Look!'

Rat squeaked like crazy and shot off Raven Boy's head, as the pirate made a lunge for him.

Raven Boy stepped back, and dropped a pineapple, which suddenly appeared on deck.

'Ooo!' said the pirate. 'A pineapple!'

His friends were not so excited.

'There's something aboard the *Sea Dragon*,' one cried.

'A ghost! Some monster from the Scream Sea!' said another.

'Ah . . .' said Elf Girl.

'No!' cried Raven Boy, too loud.

'Who said that?' yelled the pirates.

'Ah . . .' said Elf Girl again.

'Who said that?' roared Blackblood.

'Choo!' sneezed Elf Girl, and suddenly appeared in a flurry of grapefruit, ship's biscuits and orange squash bottles, all falling from under her dress and rolling across the deck.

'Oh, nuts,' said Raven Boy.

The pirates lunged at Elf Girl and grabbed her, but three of them ran slap bang into the still invisible Raven Boy.

'What?' they cried, and then Raven Boy began to feel his nose tickle.

'Oh, nuts again,' he said. And then, 'Ah-choo!'

He appeared too, and a whole cheese rolled away down the deck, followed by a watermelon.

'Right!' roared Blackblood. 'Stowaways! Keel-haul 'em! Hang 'em from the main mast! Make 'em walk the plank! Feed 'em to the fishes!'

Within seconds, the pirates had set up a gang-plank, leading off the side of the ship, high above the water.

Elf Girl and Raven Boy were shoved onto the end of the plank and Blackblood whipped out his cutlass and waved it in their faces.

'Stow away on my ship, would you?' he snarled. 'I'll show you what happens to stowaways! Walk the plank and take your chances with the beasties, or I'll cut you both in half at once.'

Elf Girl and Raven Boy looked at each other, and edged towards the end of the plank, which was wobbling over the sea like the jelly they'd tried to eat the night before.

'Come on, you smelly swabs!' roared Blackblood. 'We don't have all—'

But he never finished what he was saying because, at that very moment, a long tentacle, as wide as a tree trunk and covered in horrid-looking suckers, swept up and out of the sea and plucked Blackblood into the sky.

He screeched as he flew through the air with the tentacle holding him tight.

Everyone whirled round and then the thing that owned the tentacle stuck its head out of the water. It had about thirteen eyes, a beak like an eagle but the size of a house, and was covered in green and orange slime. It opened its mouth and popped Blackblood inside, in one go. Just like that.

Everyone watched silently, and then, all at once, began screaming.

Nineteen

**True troll fact: Trolls are very stupid,
so stupid they have no idea how dumb
they actually are.**

'Captain!' wailed the pirates, running around
in crazy circles.

Raven Boy and Elf Girl were immediately
forgotten in the panic, and ran back on board ship.

'Well, that was a piece of luck!' cried
Elf Girl. 'Thank goodness that monster ate the
captain.'

'Yes!' agreed Raven Boy. 'That should
keep it busy for a while.'

Then he screamed.

Elf Girl turned to see another tentacle
rising from the water, and then another, and
another.

'It's back!' wailed Elf Girl.

'And it's more than it! There's lots of them!'

They could see at least three of the sea beasties now, their heads poking out of the water, as they began to try and grab a nice pirate snack.

'What do we do?' cried Elf Girl.

'I don't know!' said Raven Boy. He looked around desperately. 'Hide! The crow's nest!'

It wasn't a bad idea to get as high as possible, and as far away from the tentacles as they could. Elf Girl set a new personal climbing record, and then she and Raven Boy sat and watched the chaos below. Rat, who had climbed back into Raven Boy's pocket for safety, wasn't watching. He had his paws over his eyes and was trying to pretend nothing bad was happening.

The pirates had stopped running around wildly and were now trying to fight back. They had cutlasses and swords and pikes and some even had long rifles with which they were trying to shoot the tentacles. The beasties writhed and wriggled but, one by one, the pirates were being sucked up and over the side of the ship, into the mouths of the hungry monsters.

'Maybe they don't know we're up here!'
Elf Girl whispered, hopefully, but then things
got worse.

There was a huge banging sound, like
the beating of a massive drum, and as Raven
Boy and Elf Girl stared at each other, the whole
ship began to shudder.

'They're trying to break the hull!' cried
Raven Boy. Then there was another massive
underwater thud, and a terrible cracking sound,
as the ship started to break in two.

'Oh! Oh, we're sinking!' Raven Boy screamed.

'Raven Boy!' shouted Elf Girl. 'I think it might be time to blow Molo's whistle, don't you?'

'Yes! Yes!' Raven Boy said, and fumbled to find the shell. Very carefully, he put it to his lips.

'Hurry!' cried Elf Girl. 'We'll be in the water in a second!'

The ship was going under fast and their crow's nest was sinking quickly towards the sea, which was full of tentacles and pirates.

'Hurry!'

Raven Boy blew the whistle.

Nothing happened. At least, there was no sound.

'Did you do it right?' asked Elf Girl.

'I have no idea,' said Raven Boy, shrugging.

'Do it again! Quickly!'

He did, and again there was no sound, just the faintest whisper of air blowing through the tiny shell.

'That's it!' sighed Elf Girl. 'We're dead!'

The crow's nest was almost in the water.

Raven Boy and Elf Girl clung to each other, and Rat moved out of Raven Boy's pocket and stood on tippy-toes on Raven Boy's head, trying to get as far away from the sea for as long as he could.

But it was no good, and down they went.

Raven Boy shut his eyes, waiting to either drown or be sucked to bits by a monster. Suddenly something grabbed his wrists, and he began to move through the water at an incredible speed.

He opened his eyes, and saw Molo holding his right wrist. On his left was another mermaid, also holding him and whizzing him along. Two more mermaids had Elf Girl, and a fifth held Rat carefully in both hands.

The mermaids broke the surface of the sea, back into the air. The sinking ship, the pirates and the sea monsters were already far behind them.

'Breathe!' cried Molo, and they all took a deep breath, before the mermaids dived again and swam underwater for another minute or two.

By the time they came up once more, the ship was out of sight.

'Wow!' cried Raven Boy. 'You're so fast!'

'You came!' said Elf Girl, happily. 'Thank you!'

Rat squeaked and the mermaids giggled.

'Take another breath!' Molo told them.

They went underwater once more, and zoomed along, so fast that Raven Boy could hardly believe it.

As the sun started to set, they came in sight of land, and a port.

The mermaids rose for the last time.

'Waterspout,' Molo said. 'You'll be safe here.'

'Thank you!' cried Raven Boy. 'You saved us!'

'As you saved me! I promised we would. Now, please may I have my shell back? It's time for us to go and I might need to give it to someone else, one day.'

Raven Boy handed her the shell, and the mermaids swam away.

'Well,' he said. 'Waterspout!'

Elf Girl nodded, and they began to paddle slowly towards the docks.

As they climbed out of the water, they found they were standing by a large ship.

'Raven Boy,' said Elf Girl slowly. 'Does that look familiar to you?'

Raven Boy looked up at the ship.

It did look familiar.

He read its name.

The *Naughty Porpoise*.

'Scrim!' cried Elf Girl. 'My bow!'

'Elf Girl . . . ' began Raven Boy, but it was too late. She was already marching up the gang-plank.

Twenty

Raven Boy is braver than he thinks he is.
He argues back with Elf Girl, something
her own family don't dare to do.

Raven Boy just about managed to grab Elf
Girl and get her to calm down before she
walked straight on board and into Scrim's
clutches.

Her ears were going pink and he knew
he was taking a risk, but he pulled her off the
gang-plank and back to the side of the dock.

'I want my bow!' said Elf Girl, crossly.

'I know. I want you to have it too,' said

Raven Boy. 'But maybe there's a better way to go about it. Let's have a sneak about, yes?'

'Okay,' said Elf Girl, grumpily.

So they did.

They crept along the dock, peering through the portholes of the ship. Everything seemed very quiet, as if no one was aboard, but then they came to the far end, and heard low voices.

Raven Boy peered through the porthole, and sat back down suddenly.

'You're not going to believe this,' he said.

Elf Girl stood up and had a peek.

'You're right,' she said, sitting back down. 'I don't.'

But it was true.

There, inside Captain Scrim's cabin, were not only the captain and the crew, but also the three trolls who'd been following them since they first set out to find Fright Forest. Being daytime still, the trolls were in the form of men, but Raven Boy and Elf Girl knew them all too well, whichever form they were in.

'Listen!' whispered Elf Girl.

Scrim was just telling the crew how lucky they were to have caught three new slaves to sell on Blackheart Isle.

'Did you see my bow?' whispered Elf Girl.

'Yes, it's on the captain's desk!' said Raven Boy. 'But never mind that for now. The pirates don't know what they've got there.'

Raven Boy was right. Scrim and the pirates had the three trolls tied up with rope around their wrists.

'Take them below!' Scrim was telling his crew. 'And set sail!'

'No!' whispered Elf Girl. 'We can't let them go!'

'We won't have to!' said Raven Boy, smiling. 'Look!'

He pointed to where the sun was setting, back to the west, over the sea.

'Raven Boy!' cried Elf Girl.

Just as the sun set, they heard some strange noises from inside the cabin, and peered inside, to see the trolls turning from men, back

into trolls. They'd seen it once before, but it was still an incredible and, to be honest, unpleasant sight to see.

The pirates didn't think it was unpleasant, because they were too busy screaming, a screaming which got worse as the trolls casually snapped their ropes as if they were cotton.

There was a stampede as the pirates fled from the cabin back onto deck and ran off into the town, whimpering like small dogs, with the trolls hard on their heels.

'Well,' said Elf Girl, standing up. 'Shall we?'

'Why not?' agreed Raven Boy, and they sauntered on board, into the captain's cabin, and took Elf Girl's bow.

'Would it be wrong to take this too?' Raven Boy asked, holding up a small bag of coins.

'I think they owe us that much, at least,' said Elf Girl, 'for scaring us and for taking my bow.'

'Good point,' said Raven Boy.

'So! Let's go and save the world again! Find the Singing Sword and the Tears of the Moon, and then save the world.'

'Right,' said Raven Boy. 'But let's find something to eat first, yes?'

He jingled the bag of coins.

Elf Girl laughed.

'All right, Ravenous Boy. You're on.'

Next

Follow Raven Boy and Elf Girl (and Rat) as they head out towards DREAD DESERT . . .

FRIGHT FOREST

MONSTER MOUNTAINS

SCREAM SEA

DREAD DESERT

TERROR TOWN

CREEPY CAVES

IF YOU ENJOYED SCREAM SEA YOU'LL LOVE MARCUS SEDGWICK'S OTHER SERIES FOR YOUNGER READERS, THE RAVEN MYSTERIES.

Meet Valevine the inventor, Minty who was once a witch, gorgeous, glum Solstice, her little brother Cudweed and his monkey, Fellah, and Edgar the raven, their self-appointed Guardian.

MARCUS SEDGWICK
FLOOD
AND FANG
The Raven Mysteries

'Nobody likes a sticky monkey'

Edgar's alarmed when a nasty looking black tail
slinks off under the rhubarb, kitchen maids go
missing and the castle begins to flood. It won't be
long before the Otherhands come face to face with
the owner of the black tail.

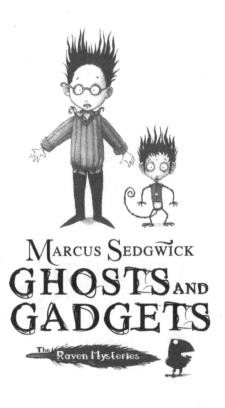

MARCUS SEDGWICK
GHOSTS AND GADGETS

The Raven Mysteries

'Does my beak look wonky?'

Edgar is so preoccupied that when Cudweed sees a guh . . . a guh . . . You-Know-What, Edgar almost forgets that he's the Guardian of Otherhand Castle. But the rumblings and wailing from the Lost South Wing can no longer be ignored. It's up to Solstice and Edgar to go ghost-hunting, and pit their wits against the obnoxious Captain Spookini.

Marcus Sedgwick
LUNATICS AND LUCK

The Raven Mysteries

'This sort of stuff can bend your brain fairly rapidly.'

Full moons and money troubles are nothing out of
the ordinary at Castle Otherhand. But add a
horrible, hairy, howling new school teacher,
complete with mysterious heavy wooden trunk, and
the earth trembles and the body count rises.
Solstice and Cudweed are at his mercy. Gasp!

MARCUS SEDGWICK
VAMPIRES AND VOLTS
The Raven Mysteries

'Pumpkin brains everywhere!'

It's Halloween and the Otherhands are throwing a
Vampire Party . . . in the midst of which, the lights
go out, and the ballroom is plunged into darkness.
What happens next could only happen to them!
Thank goodness Edgar is there to swoop to the
rescue.

Marcus Sedgwick
MAGIC AND
MAYHEM

The Raven Mysteries

'A bored bird is a dangerous bird'

Following a family outing to the circus, Minty falls
under the spell of a dodgy fortune-teller, Castle
Otherhand is overrun by furry white bunnies, a
mucky duck and a hamster called Mr Whiskers, and
Valevine creates a strangely lethal cabbage-counting
contraption. Rark! The Castle is in mayhem.

Marcus Sedgwick
DIAMONDS
and DOOM

The Raven Mysteries

'My beak nearly bent with surprise!'

Castle Otherhand is up for sale. Minty, Lord
Valevine, Solstice, Cudweed and even Fellah are at
their wit's end. Chaos and catastrophe reign, and
there's only hours left to get rid of a mystical space
time vortex thingummy, save everyone from whatever is roaming the corridors, and find a squillion or
two in cash.

the
orion star